PENNY

HANDS I PASSED THROUGH - THINGS I SAW

STORIES I CAN TELL!

PENNY

Hands I Passed Through - Things I Saw
Stories I Can Tell!

Peter Davidson

SWEET MEMORIES PUBLISHING

A Division of Sweet Memories, Inc.

sweetmemories@mchsi.com

Copyright © 2017 by Peter Davidson

ISBN: 978-0-9762718-9-5
Library of Congress Control Number: 2017904976
First printing, June, 2017

Published by Sweet Memories Publishing

PRINTED IN THE UNITED STATES OF AMERICA

10 9 8 7 6 5 4 3 2 1

Acknowledgments

Editor: Wordright Services

Front Cover Art: Jason Tako

Back Cover Photo: David Devary

Graphic Design: Debbie Wilson

Readers: Beverly Peterson, Barbara Schomaker,
Clark Marshall, W. T. Heil,
Nancy Schendel, Don Mitchell,
Diane Olson, Dan Trowse, Jeff Brown,
Russ Pouliot, Judy Pouliot, Skip Moore,
John Smith, Cathy Edam

Dedicated
to
The *Penny Pinchers* of the World

Table of Contents

Way Beyond Ordinary

Hi, I'm Penny. I've been around. I've basked in the sunshine and I've been in the deepest of darkness. I've been prized and hungered for and, on the other hand, I've been scorned, ridiculed, pinched, squeezed, ignored, hoarded, stepped on, driven on by cars, and threatened with total annihilation and extinction.

Penny is actually my nickname. Officially, the U.S. Mint's name for me is "Cent" and the U.S. Treasury's name for me is "One-Cent Piece." I prefer to be called Penny. Like other inanimate objects like a hammer, computer, bottle, clock, building, or desk, I am neither male nor female. I have no gender, so please think of me as gender neutral. If it will help you out on that issue, you can call me by the Italian translation of my name, Centesimo.

I was born, or "minted," on a very special day, October 22, 1982 in Denver, Colorado. The reason this is such a special day, and that I am so special – not an ordinary One-Cent Piece – is that I was the final penny to be made on that day and the final penny ever to be made of 95% copper, with just a touch of zinc thrown in. All birth announcements list weight, length, and so on, so here's mine: when minted, I weighed 3.11 grams, was .75 inches in diameter, and was .0598 inches thick.

After my birth date, all new one-cent pieces are pathetic,

consisting of 97.5% zinc and only 2.5% copper and weighing a puny 2.5 grams. I am the last of the real deal.

My front, or "Obverse," has the image of Abraham Lincoln, and the back side, or "Reverse," has the image of the Lincoln Memorial. The Mint has messed around with all sorts of images on the Reverse starting in 2009.

I tell you the information listed above simply so you can get a firm image of me in your mind as I tell you my story. And, what a story it is. I traveled widely and met people from all walks of life including ordinary people, the famous, the infamous, the saints, and the sinners. I hung out in churches and honkytonks and everywhere in between. And, all the while, I was watching and listening, and that's what my story is about – everything I saw and heard as I was passed around from one person to another. You probably don't remember me, but I may have passed through your fingers and one of the stories I am about to tell may very well be about you. But, worry not - I changed the names and your secret is safe with me - wink, wink.

Out into the Cold, Cruel, Wonderful World

After I was minted, I was placed in a paper roll with forty-nine other freshly-minted one-cent pieces; I'm the last one at the end of the roll. The roll was placed in a box and the box was placed on top of a stack of boxes.

A few days later, our box is placed in an armored truck and hauled to the Great Western Bank in Littleton, Colorado. There, a pretty young thing grabs our roll, slams it against the edge of the counter until the paper wrapper breaks, and pours us into a drawer with some other, older, beat-up, and tarnished one-cent pieces. When I get to be 50, 100, or 200 years old, I hope I never end up looking like them.

A preppy-looking guy, about thirty, comes in with a check made out to Andrew Wilmont for $446.41 and asks for cash. The pretty young thing grabs some bills along with a quarter, dime, nickel – and me – and hands it to Andrew. He stuffs the bills in his billfold and dumps me and the other coins in his pocket. We walk out of the bank into the cool mountain air.

I'm on my way!

Andrew gets into his car - a 1979 Datsun 280 ZX. Within minutes we're on Interstate 70, heading west. Maybe we're going to Vail, maybe Breckenridge. Just before we get to Idaho Springs, though, Andrew turns off and we're on a winding two-lane mountain road. And then, we're there – The Grand Hotel in Central City.

Andrew checks in and heads straight to the hotel's bar, where he orders a Crown Royal and Coke and joins two buddies who are already seated at a corner table. Their conversation centers around tomorrow's mountain climbing excursion.

A tall, leggy blonde enters the room, takes a seat at the bar, and orders a margarita. Andrew is mesmerised by her. He reaches in his pocket, sorts through his change, clinches me in his fist and grabs his cocktail in his other hand. "Watch this," he says to his buddies.

Andrew walks over to The Blonde, holds his fist in front of her eyes, and slowly unclinches it, revealing me in all of my newly minted glory. The Blonde looks at me and smiles.

"A penny for your thoughts..." Andrew says.

Gawd, is that cheesy.

Lightning fast, The Blonde scoops me from Andrew's hand. Her hand is warm and soft.

The Blonde raises her cocktail glass in front of Andrew's eyes and says, "I propose a toast." Andrew is cocky, self-assured, arrogant, smooth. That old Wilmont charm is working like magic.

The Blonde says, "Mine's up, so up yours." Suddenly, she grabs the front of Andrew's pants, gives them a tug, and pours her drink down his pants. Andrew stands there in shock, with his pants dripping wet, while his buddies laugh hilariously.

The Blonde hustles away, with me in her hot little hand.

A short time later, The Blonde orders a hot chocolate at the hotel coffee shop, which costs $1.25. She sorts through the bills and change in her wallet, hands the clerk the exact amount of the purchase, $1.25, drops a dollar in the tip jar – and to my utter disappointment, drops me in the "Leave a Penny – Take a Penny" dish.

A half hour later, a middle-aged man dressed in a suit, pale blue shirt, and red tie orders a black coffee and a chocolate chip cookie at the coffee shop. He notices me in the penny dish. In fact, he can't take his eyes off of me. Why not – after all, I am the newest, freshest, prettiest one in the dish. When the clerk's back is turned to get his coffee, the man grabs me from the dish and slips me into his pocket. He pays the clerk and gets change back including three pennies, which he dumps in the penny dish. He paid three times my face value for me but, after all, I am special, you know.

The next day, the well-dressed gentleman and I are on the road early, leaving Central City at 6 a.m. Around 8 a.m. we pull into a convenience store in Colorado Springs. The man buys a doughnut and a medium coffee. When he reaches the car, he pulls his keys out of his pocket – I'm caught in the key ring and, Whoosh, I'm flying through the air and Bang! I hit the cement parking lot. He's trying to juggle his cup of coffee, doughnut, and keys and doesn't see me. He gets in his car, and away he goes, leaving me lie there.

Boom! A pickup truck drives his big front tire right on

top of me. It doesn't hurt because I am an inanimate object – but, dammit, it hurts my pride. Minutes later, the pickup backs up and runs over me again. For the next forty-five minutes I'm driven on by a variety of cars, trucks, motorcycles, a bicycle, and five people who stepped on me and never even knew it. One guy looked down, saw me, and muttered to himself, "It's only a penny."

What a Dick.

Finally, a fellow, maybe seventy years old, spots me and stoops over, slowly, to pick me up. As stiff as he is, I don't think he'll be able to reach me, and if he does, I doubt he'll be able to get back up without someone helping him. As it turns out, he is unable to reach me, so he drops to his knees, picks me up, and uses the fender of the car next to him to pull himself up to his feet. He is almost exhausted. I feel proud – he went through all that just for me.

About ten hours later, I reach my new home, in Lincoln, Nebraska. The trip yesterday from Littleton to Central City and today from Central City to Colorado Springs was scenic and fun. Today, I couldn't help but notice – Nebraska is as flat as a pancake.

The elderly gentleman walks into the house, goes straight to a room, and turns on the light. There are eight shelves that run the entire length of the wall and what is resting on those shelves gives me the same feeling that a person must get when a judge sentences them to life in prison, without parole. There are perhaps two hundred plastic gallon jars, all filled with pennies. I had been scooped up from that convenience store parking lot by a penny hoarder – a damned penny hoarder.

The old guy reaches in his pocket and pulls out his change, including three other pennies and me. He throws us into a jar that is half full, turns out the light, walks out, and shuts the door.

So, this is how my life will be for the next ten or twenty years until the old guy croaks and his heirs haul all of us off to the bank in a wheelbarrow. I want *action* – I want to go places, do things, meet people, have some fun. And here I sit. Within a week or two, the old guy will come up with enough pennies to bury me and in a few months, the jar will be full and he'll put the lid on the jar and that will be it.

I can hear them out there, a whole bunch of them, talking and laughing and having a big time while I and several hundred thousand of my ancestors are sitting here in these jars on these shelves. I've only been here two days but it feels like it's been months.

Suddenly, the door to the room slowly opens. A small figure creeps into the room in a crouch and quietly shuts the door. It's a boy, maybe nine years old. He heads straight for the shelves in the dark – the little scamp has been here before. His hands glide along the jars until he comes to the last one – my jar. He reaches his little hand into the jar and grabs a fistful of pennies, including me. He drops us into his pants pocket and slowly makes his way out of the room.

I have been saved! I like this little rascal. I don't know what he has in mind, but I'll betcha he's not going to put me in a jar in his room. Within a day, he'll be in a store buying candy or bubble gum and I'll be back in circulation. I *love* this little rascal.

The little rascal puts me and the other pennies he took from the jar in a sock, ties it, and places the sock, and us, in his back pack.

The next morning we're off to school. The little rascal, whose name turns out to be Billy, has been called on three times by the teacher and the only way to describe him is to say he is *clueless,* and that is being generous. The entire class is a bunch of unruly and antsy jabber mouths who can't sit still and who cannot keep quiet. The teacher looks like she is on the verge of a nervous breakdown.

Billy and two of his buddies have a quick lunch in the school cafeteria, hustle outside, and gather beside a big tree behind the school building. Here, Billy and each of his buddies reach into their pockets and each withdraws a fistful of pennies. They each select a penny and dump the rest back into their pockets. They all flip their penny in the air, catch it, and slap it down on their forehead. Two have heads and one has tails; the one with tails wins and takes the other two boys' pennies. Billy is one of the losers and he reaches in his pocket and selects me. He gives me a kiss and flips me in the air. I come up heads and both of the other boys' pennies are tails; Billy wins their pennies. Billy, and I win the next four rounds and Billy's pocket is starting to bulge with his winnings. We're a great team. We're going to wipe these guys out. The school bell rings and lunch hour is over – back to class.

The classroom is as chaotic as it was before the lunch

break until a stern-looking woman knocks on the door and summons the teacher. The classroom falls totally silent. Something big is up. The teacher turns to face the class and announces, "The Principal would like to see Billy, Thomas, and Gerard, in his office immediately." It's the three penny flippers. Billy's face goes pale and his knees start to wobble.

The stern woman takes Billy and the other two boys to the Principal's office and shuts the door behind them. The Principal looks them over with eyes of stone and gets right down to business. "I understand you boys have been gambling on school property – is that true?" "No, No, No," they all answer in unison in quivering voices.

The Principal stares at them for a moment, "Empty your pockets," he commands in a gruff voice. Slowly, they reach into their pockets and deposit their pennies on the Principal's desk.

The Principal stares at the three piles of pennies and then glares at the three gamblers. They all look down, afraid to look the Principal in the eye. Finally, the Principal speaks, "If I ever catch any of you gambling again on school property, or anywhere else, I'm going to call your parents first and then I'm going to call the police. Do you understand?"

"Yes, Yes, Yes," the boys repeat in unison. Two of them have already peed in their pants and the other one is on the verge of passing out.

"Good," the Principal says. "You can go back to class now." The boys scramble out of the Principal's office and hustle down the hallway to their class.

The stern woman, who witnessed the action from the back of the office, slowly closes the Principal's door. She and the Principal look at each other and burst into laughter. "You probably saved those boys from a life of crime," she says and the two of them howl in laughter.

ooooo

The Principal is in the local drug store. He asks the clerk, "How much is a pack of Blackjack gum?" She replies, "Thirty-five cents." The Principal frowns.

"Is the manager in?" the Principal asks.

"Yes," the clerk says - "that's him over there in the white shirt."

"I was wondering," the Principal says to the manager, "if you'd make me a deal on this pack of Blackjack gum." The manager looks at the Principal with a blank stare on his face that seems to say, "Huh?"

The Principal reaches into his pocket and produces a fistful of pennies, including me. "I only have thirty-four cents - will you take it for this pack of gum?"

The manager is too dumbfounded to say anything but, "Uh, ya."

The Principal dumps the pennies into the manager's hand and leaves with his pack of Blackjack gum.

See you around, big spender.

ooooo

The other thirty-three pennies and I from the gambling loot have been in the cash register for less than two minutes when a woman buys three items totaling $19.97 and gives the clerk a $20 bill. The clerk grabs me and two other pennies from the drawer, gives us to the woman, and she dumps us into the bottom of her purse.

A new adventure begins.

The woman gets into the passenger seat of the car and her husband says, "Where's my change?"

"It came to $19.97," the woman says. " You gave me a $20."

"Gimme the change," he orders.

"The three cents?" she asks.

"It's my money, dammit, and I want it," he replies gruffly as he starts to pull the car away from the curb.

The woman digs in the bottom of her purse and finds the other two pennies and me. She holds the pennies in her open hand for her husband to see. "See these three pennies," she says as she rolls down her window with the other hand.

"If you want 'em, go get 'em," she says as she flings the three of us pennies out the window. The three of us hit the side of a Buick Roadmaster parked along the curb. I land on the street about a foot from the car. One of the other pennies flies under the car and the third one rolls and rolls until it falls down the storm sewer, never to be seen again.

What a crappy way to spend the rest of your life.

The husband slams on the brakes and the tires squeal.

"What in the hell did you do that for?" he screams. "Some people don't know the value of a dollar - you don't know the value of a penny."

He tromps on the gas and the tires squeal as the car rocks from side to side as it lurches down the street.

Lady, what are you doing with that jerk?

Life in a Buick Roadmaster

My future is uncertain, lying here on the street as cars and trucks whiz by within inches. Will I lie here until the street sweeper comes along in the morning and sweeps me to the curb, or worse yet, down the storm sewer? Will some crackpot find me and relegate me to life in a piggy bank? Will some kid find me and put me on the railroad track to see if the rumor is true that the train will flatten a penny as thin as a piece of paper? Will I be driven on by a thousand cars and trucks until my beautiful shine is gone, I am full of nicks and scratches, and look like I am old long before my time? Will I …

And then, along came Charlie.

"Well, lookie here, what somebody left for good ol' Charlie – a brand new, fresh, shiny penny. Face side up – this is Charlie's lucky day."

Charlie picks me up, admires me, and gets into the Buick Roadmaster – a humongous, long, wide, heavy car with big fins and lots of chrome. It is a '58, but it still shines like, well, like a freshly-minted penny.

Charlie admires me for a moment and then he deposits me in the car's ash tray. There is nobody or nothing in here but me. I have my own private room, so to speak.

ooooo

Charlie and I have been on the road together for nearly five months now. He sells something to businesses, but I'm not sure what it is. All I know is that before every sales call Charlie pushes the "Play" button on the battery-operated tape recorder that sits on the passenger seat and a brass band plays a rousing uptempo march. Then, properly revved up, Charlie jumps out of the Roadmaster and marches off to battle with his head held high, his chest out, and a spring in his step.

An hour or two later, Charlie returns. Within five seconds of closing the car door, Charlie starts talking to himself. If things went well, he says stuff like, "Good goin' Charlie! You had 'em eating out of your hand." "They were no match for the charm and persuasive powers of Charlie Winters." "Charles D. Winters kicks ass again!" "Amateurs—they're a bunch of amateurs who were no match for super salesman Charlie Winters." "Money, money, money—did we make money today, Charlie!" "Kickin' ass and taking names—woohoo!" "Charlie, Charlie, Charlie—Man, did you do good!"

But, when things didn't go well, it is a different story. "Dickheads, what a bunch of dickheads." "I've never seen such a bunch of stupid, numbnuts in my life." "Charlie, it's a blessing in disguise that you don't have to deal with those dumbasses." "That little punk running the business his grandpa started – he'll drive it into the ground in two years and he'll be digging ditches for a living." "Technology—they want to go with *technology*. Well, it'll never last and they'll be begging

Charlie Winters to come back and bail them out and know what, Charlie Winters will tell them to stick it." "I had the sale in my pocket and was already spending my commission when they brought in that smartass accountant. What the hell does he know about numbers?" "Charlie, let's go talk to that guy's competitor and shoot him a deal he can't refuse and we'll drive that little prick out of business." "I'll get him. One way or the other, I'll get that guy." "Threw Charlie Winters out of your office, huh. Well, I've been thrown out of better places than that, Pal."

Whether Charlie had a good day or a bad day, made sales or didn't make sales, the ride home was always the same.

Charlie knew every gas station and liquor store within 150 miles that sold popcorn and Pabst Blue Ribbon beer. Charlie would get a bag of popcorn and three cans of Pabst Blue Ribbon and we'd be on our way, and by the time Charlie got home, he would be a mellow fellow.

Like clockwork, after the first can of beer and a couple fistfuls of popcorn, Charlie would start singing. It was always the same song; I think he made it up: "Granpappy used to say when you're feelin' low and ill, ain't nothin' gonna cure you like beer and popcorn will. When your head is ringing and your stomach's upside down, just take yourself some popcorn and some beer to wash it down." And then, Charlie would sing it again, and again, and again.

During the day, and sober, Charlie would often sing along with the radio, but the high notes were too high for Charlie and the low notes were too low. There were, however, three or four notes in the middle where Charlie really gave it hell. After a couple of Pabst Blue Ribbons, Charlie could hit every note when he sang "Beer and Popcorn." But then, you don't often hear a song that only has three notes.

Besides selling, popcorn, Pabst Blue Ribbon, and singing, Charlie had two great loves—his magnificent 1958 Buick Roadmaster and his sixteen-year-old son, Charlie, Jr.

According to Charlie, the Buick Roadmaster was the finest automobile ever produced. He bought it new in '58 and vowed to drive it until he died. At least that's what he told the Roadmaster every now and then. So far, he was making good on the promise, having over 178,000 miles behind him to prove his word was good.

Life on the road for a traveling salesman can be a lonely business with no one to talk to except customers who you don't really talk to as much as you do battle with them. But, Charlie has two good friends to talk to—himself and the Roadmaster, who he addresses as "Roady."

"Roady, see that Chevy up there – let's blow his doors off." "Roady, look at that cheap foreign job – they make the fenders out of tin cans." "Good move, Roady - wow, any other car taking that curve at 80 would be laying in the ditch in a heap." "You just can't beat the way a Roadmaster rides. Finest car ever made."

And then, there's Charlie, Jr.

ooooo

Charlie had only one car, his beloved "Roady," and when it came time for Charlie, Jr. to drive, there was only one choice – he would drive the Roadmaster.

It was summertime, Charlie, Jr. was sixteen, and now that he had access to a set of wheels, his dating stock had improved and he had a girlfriend. Candy was seventeen and had a lot of similarities to the Roadmaster – she looked great and had a lot of miles on her.

Junior and Candy had been dating for two months now. At first they went to a movie or went roller skating and would make out parked in the driveway in front of Candy's house. For the past three weeks, though, they have skipped the preliminaries and head straight for a little-used gravel road out in the country two nights a week. They park the car and scramble into the massive back seat of the Roadmaster, that is bigger and roomier than a single bed. Perfect.

Candy is Junior's first girlfriend, so he has no previous backseat experience whatsoever. Candy, on the other hand, confessed that she has been dating since she was fourteen and "has been around the block a few times."

Candy and Junior have been grinding away on each other, with their clothes on, for the past two weeks. Junior is filled with lust and wants to go all the way but he is scared as hell. Candy has been ready for action since the second or third date and has been hinting that if Junior doesn't get it going pretty soon she'll find someone who will.

They are in the back seat grinding away, kissing madly,

moaning and groaning, when Candy whispers in Junior's ear, "The zipper's in the back."

Charlie Jr. can't hold it back any longer—he throws caution to the wind, two zippers fly down at lightning speed, and Junior goes for it . . . .

WHAMO! Candy screams and Junior moans. "Wow! I've never had a climax like that in my life!" Candy yells.

From my vantage point in the ash tray, I know what has happened before the dazed lovers figure it out, and Junior had nothing to do with it. We have been rear ended by a cement truck and the Roadmaster, now about eight feet shorter than it was just a moment ago, is in the ditch. The back of the Roadmaster is crumpled up like one of the Pabst Blue Ribbon beer cans that Charlie smashes against his forehead before he tosses it out of the car window. The front end, which came to rest against a steel culvert, didn't fare much better.

The driver of the cement truck is unharmed and Junior and Candy, protected by the backrest of the Roadmaster's back seat, didn't suffer even a scratch. But, how to tell Charlie, Sr. and what to tell him.

To his credit, Charlie Sr. asks the right question first, "Was anybody hurt?" Upon hearing that everyone is okay, he asks the dreaded second question, "Was the, was the Roadmaster, ah, was it hurt?"

Bob, from Bob's Auto Body and Wrecker Service answers Charlie's question with two words, "It's totaled."

"It can't be fixed?" Charlie asks with hope in his quivering voice.

Again, Bob gets right to the point, "No."

"What's going to happen to it?" Charlie asks with tears in his eyes.

"Louie's Auto Salvage will come get it and they'll run it through their car crusher. They're really good; when they get done the car will be the size of a suitcase," Bob says, without an ounce of sugarcoating. "Then, they'll melt it down and some day it might be recycled into a couple of fenders for one of those foreign cars."

Charlie falls to his knees. His beloved 1958 Roadmaster, "Roady," was no more. He had lost his traveling companion, his confidant, and his friend.

I'm sorry, Charlie, and Roady, too. You both deserved better. Thanks for the miles and thanks for the smiles—and remember - When you're feelin' low and ill, ain't nothin' gonna cure you like beer and popcorn will.

All the while they're standing there talking about the Roadmaster, they forgot about me. I'm still in the ash tray. If the Roadmaster gets crushed, so will I. If the Roadmaster gets melted down, so will I.

Hey, can anybody hear me? Get me out of here!

ooooo

Bob, the body shop guy, knows every angle of his business and knows that car owners often leave change or items of value tucked away in consoles, glove compartments, the trunk, or other compartments that they forget about when

19

cloaked in grief over the demise of their beloved automobile. Bob scrounged through the Roadmaster and came up with a pair of binoculars, a battery-operated tape recorder, two pair of sunglasses, a Rand McNally Atlas, a half bottle of mouthwash containing 40% alcohol that Charlie used to take a swig of before a sales call, and me. I was saved.

Bob put the items he found in the Roadmaster, including me, into an open shoebox and placed it on the corner of his desk. I have been here with this odd collection of companions for about three weeks, listening to "car guys" talk about motors, windshields, transmissions, fenders, and women, when a guy named Allan walks in.

Allan is from California and was involved in an accident when passing through town. Bob put a rush job on fixing the car and got it done in one day and Allan was there to pick up the car and continue on to California. As Allan is writing his check for the damage, he spots the box of stuff from the Roadmaster. "What's all this stuff?" he asks Bob.

"That was from a Roadmaster that was totaled about three weeks ago. I always put that stuff in a box for the owner in case they come to claim it. If they don't claim it in two or three weeks I give it away or I keep it if there's anything of interest to me. The rest I throw away. Do you want anything in the box?" Bob asks.

"Well, there's a couple of things I wouldn't mind having," Allan said.

"Then take the whole box," Bob says.

ooooo

I am now sitting in a box in the back seat of a white 1983 Cadillac Eldorado touring coupe convertible with red leather interior. Life is looking up. California, here I come!

California, Sun, Sand, and Rock "n" Roll

Allan is driving like someone is chasing him. If there is a speed limit, he either doesn't know or doesn't care. We have been on the road for eighteen hours straight and have stopped only for gas and for Allan to pee. Allan is young, maybe in his mid to late twenties. He has a baseball cap pulled low and wears sunglasses, even at night. He has been living on candy bars, root beer, and loud Rock and Roll music on the radio. Occasionally Allan beats out the rhythm of a song with his hands on the dash and steering wheel, and finishes off the drum roll using the rear view mirror for a mighty cymbal crash. Every now and then, he starts to sing along with a song and then he abruptly stops. His voice is a little hoarse – he must have a cold.

We roar through Nebraska, Wyoming, Utah, Nevada, and into California. Allan is apparently on a mission and doesn't even slow down going through Las Vegas. And now, we are here—bright sunshine, palm trees gently swaying in the breeze, and beaches filled with muscle men and girls in bikinis. Los Angeles.

Allan pulls the Caddy into a parking lot behind a small block building with a flat roof, pops the lid of the trunk, grabs a guitar case, and enters the building. As he flings open the door, people inside shout greetings to him and a few whistle and clap their hands.

A few minutes later, Allan returns and grabs the box containing the loot from the Roadmaster, including me.

He carries us into the building, which turns out to be a professional recording studio. There are two main rooms – the studio where the musicians are setting up to play and the control room filled with all sorts of electronic equipment, playback speakers, a recording engineer, and a producer.

The first thing I learn is that Allan isn't his name after all; he is Mookey. That's what everybody calls him – Mookey.

Mookey sets the box down and says, "If you see anything you want, help yourself."

Five long-haired guys wearing loud shirts and tight pants grab items from the box until it is almost empty. In fact, it is empty except for me.

"What, nobody wants the penny?" Mookey says. "Well, I'll take it – it's gonna be my good luck charm."

Mookey takes me from the box and puts his hand into his pants pocket to deposit me there, and then he stops and pulls his hand, and me, out of his pocket. He drops me into his shirt pocket, right next to his heart, and gives the pocket a couple of pats.

From the small talk, it is clear that Mookey had been to his sister's wedding in Okoboji, Iowa and then went on a fishing trip with his brother in Minnesota. The band is putting the finishing touches on its new album and then will be going on a 60-concert tour starting in a month.

"Okay, the party's over," a voice says over the speaker from the control room. "We've only got the studio booked for three hours and we've got two songs to knock out. Let's start with "Ain't Lovin' You No More.""

The drummer kicks off the song and the rest of the band joins in with a vengeance. Mookey is the lead singer and his voice isn't hoarse at all; it has a raspy quality and a three-octave range. He sounds an awful lot like that guy on the radio. Hell, he *is* that guy on the radio.

The producer has the band play the song over and over and over until he yells, "It's a keeper. Let's go on to "Soul City Dreamer.""

And, it starts all over again.

After the recording session, Mookey heads straight for his mansion overlooking the ocean. It has too many rooms to count, but eight bedrooms and ten bathrooms would seem to be about right. Of course, there's a pool, in the shape of a guitar, a tennis court, a basketball court, a twelve-stall garage, and a couple of out-buildings.

Mookey's bedroom is huge, with a round bed that is at least eight feet in diameter. He carefully places his diamond rings, Rolex, and me on the dresser, takes off his shoes, and flops down on the bed, fully clothed. He is exhausted and sleeps for twelve hours.

ooooo

The recording sessions continue for the next four days,

with each session lasting six hours. The result is the new album, which will be released about two weeks into the upcoming tour, which has been labeled the "Balls of Steel Tour."

ooooo

After the songs were finished for the new album, the band practiced four hours a day for two weeks at a sound proof, sound-tuned practice barn on Mookey's property. After each practice session, the band lounges by the pool, shoots hoops, drinks beer, and tells stories of the road. Even though they are huge Rock Stars, they are pretty much a bunch of normal guys. Well, except for the time a couple of them drove a 1982 Lincoln Continental into Mookey's swimming pool. And there are women, lots of women. And parties, lots of parties.

I have been in Mookey's shirt pocket constantly since he placed me there almost a month ago and I have seen it all.

ooooo

We have been on tour now for two weeks and have done concerts in Las Vegas, Phoenix, Albuquerque, Seattle, Denver, and Minneapolis. The band's first concert was held at the Thomas & Mack Center in Las Vegas, which is the arena on the University of Nevada, Las Vegas campus where the Runnin' Rebels play basketball. The arena holds over 18,000 people and the show sold out in less than an hour. The other concerts have been just as successful, if not more so.

26

The band travels in a private jet that holds the six band members and another dozen people including the road manager, sound engineer, lighting engineer, and the band's own publicity staff. Occasionally, a pretty young woman or two hitch a ride.

Tonight, the band is performing on a huge stage in a meadow two miles from Sturgis, in the Black Hills of South Dakota. It is the 45th annual Sturgis Motorcycle Rally and even though Sturgis is a small town of around 6,000 people, over 350,000 motorcyclists have converged on the area. Over 75,000 of them are in the meadow for the concert.

The crowd is going nuts, yelling and screaming for the band to take the stage. The band is backstage going through their normal pre-concert ritual, which is simple – a shot of Jack Daniels and a group chant, "Let's go kick some ass!" The band charges the stage and all hell breaks loose.

When Mookey and the guys are hanging out around Mookey's house or are in the recording studio, they're pretty close to being normal people. When they get on stage, however, they are a bunch of wild animals. Mookey stalks the stage like a possessed demon with a microphone in one hand and a bottle of Jack Daniels in the other. Before the show is over, both will be annihilated and he'll throw both of them into the audience along with anything else he can get his hands on. His soft-spoken demeanor is left backstage and on stage he is a yelling, ranting, swearing maniac, exhorting the crowd to do things that would normally get you five to ten in the pen.

Before the night is over, something is going up in smoke. In Seattle, the lead guitar player set his guitar on fire, in Denver, they set a Grand piano on fire and shoved it off the stage.

A couple of guys in the band have been joking that the stage for tonight's concert would make a fine bonfire. The stage was especially built for tonight's concert and is the biggest stage in the upper Midwest, built entirely from wood milled right in the Black Hills.

After whipping the crowd into a frenzy with "Soul City Dreamer" from the new album, Mookey starts at mid stage and runs full speed to the front of the stage and dives headfirst into the crowd. Concertgoers grab Mookey and abruptly stop his forward progress, but I fly out of Mookey's shirt pocket like I have been shot out of a slingshot. He doesn't even know I'm gone.

A couple of biker women see me fly through the air and grab for me, knocking me to the ground. They drop to their knees and search for me in the dirt with their hands. Finally, one of them grabs me and yells, "I've got it." The other biker woman grabs her by the hair and tries to wrestle me from her grip. The first biker woman punches her in the nose and kicks her in the shin and that ends that.

The biker woman gives me to her biker man and says, "Put this in your pocket, I'm going to have an earring made out of it."

And, that's how my career in Rock and Roll ended. Goodbye, Mookey. Keep Rockin'.

ooooo

It is the morning after the concert, the fire department has finally gotten the fire that burned down the stage under control and Biker Man, Biker Babe, and I are on Main Street Sturgis. They are looking for a jewelry store to get a hole drilled in me to make an earring for Biker Babe. Life is fickle, even for a penny. Yesterday I flew into town in a private jet and took the stage with one of the hottest rock bands on the planet. Today, I'll be flapping in the wind hanging from Biker Babe's ear on the back of a motorcycle.

There are thousands of motorcycles sitting along the entire length of Main Street and lining every side street as far as you can see. Police, many of whom are reinforcements brought in from Chicago and New York City for the Rally, patrol the streets in groups of four.

Biker Man and Biker Babe find a jewelry store and approach the counter. Biker Man reaches in his pocket and pulls out his change – he has two quarters, a dime, a nickel – and two bright, shiny pennies. Biker Babe looks at the coins in his hand and says, "You dumb shit. Which one is Mookey's penny?"

The other penny is also a 1982, bearing the Denver mint mark, just like me. We may look identical, but I am actually shinier and prettier, and recall that I am very special.

Biker Babe looks the two of us pennies over and finally decides that the other one was Mookey's penny.

There is a God.

The jeweler drills a hole in the unlucky penny, threads an earring hoop through it and Biker Babe hangs it from her ear.

Nice.

Biker Man pays the jeweler for drilling the hole and gives him his remaining coins, including me, as a tip.

The jeweler drops the coins, including me, into his cash register. It feels good in here, safe. But I probably won't be here for long.

Passed Around Like a Hot Potato

The bikers at the Sturgis Motorcycle Rally come from all walks of life, from every state in the U.S., and from many foreign countries. They all have a few things in common—they're here to ride their bikes through the numerous winding two lane roads in the Black Hills, to party, to socialize, and to spend lots of money on clothes, souvenirs, and whatever fits their fancy.

I spend less than a minute in the jewelry store cash register before being handed to a former steel worker from Pittsburgh who is at his tenth Rally. He hops on his bike and takes me to Custer, where I end up in the cash register at a restaurant specializing in homemade pies.

From there, I am passed to a female literary agent from San Francisco to a lawyer from Miami to a hog farmer from Missouri to a college professor from Vermont to a truck driver from Indiana to a oil field worker from Texas to a Broadway actor from New York City to a chef from New Orleans to a nurse from Arizona to a seamstress from Maryland and to a state Senator from Idaho. And, that is just in the morning.

I eventually end up in the pocket of a great big biker man who rides from Hill City, where he got me, to Deadwood, at record-shattering speed. The main street of Deadwood resembles the main street of Sturgis – bikes everywhere.

Big Biker Man heads straight for Saloon No. 10, which features the chair that Wild Bill Hickok was sitting in when he was shot to death while holding the poker "Death Hand" of aces and eights. Saloon No. 10 also features busts of other famous Deadwood residents from the gold rush days of 1876, including Calamity Jane, Potato Creek Johnny, and Poker Alice.

The place is packed and Big Biker Man bullies his way up to the bar and orders a "Double Jack with a Coke back." He slams the whiskey, takes a swig of the cola and orders another round. He has five rounds in twenty minutes, which would have leveled most boozers, but Big Biker Man seems unfazed. When he reaches in his pocket for cash to buy his sixth round, he finds he is broke. He walks out of the bar and when he gets to the sidewalk, he reaches in his front pocket, grabs all of his change, including me, and flings us out into the street. "There," he yells, "now I'm really broke," and he promptly passes out.

I hit a parked motorcycle and bounce back onto the sidewalk, where a biker wannabe wearing a leather jacket, dress pants, and street shoes picks me up. My first thought is, *"Thanks for rescuing me."* My second thought is, *"Dude, do you realize you're at the Sturgis Motorcycle Rally?"*

Biker Dude puts me in the coin compartment of his billfold, and I am glad to be there. My biggest fear when being passed around from one person to another at the Sturgis Rally is that I'll end up with one of the bikers from England,

Germany, Australia, Ireland, or Italy who would take me back to their country as a souvenir and I'll spend eternity in a foreign land.

I catch a glimpse of Biker Dude's driver's license when he puts me in his billfold. He is Michael Hargrove from Ohio. Biker Dude may be a misfit at the rally, and most likely he isn't as exciting as Mookey, but I wouldn't mind spending a little time in Ohio.

Heading to the Big House?

Biker Dude, Michael Hargrove, is back in his element in Ohio. He is wearing a nice suit, blue shirt, and gray tie when he reports for work Monday morning.

As soon, as he walks in the door of the office, an older gentleman says, "Mike step in my office for a minute."

Mike enters the roomy, nicely appointed office and the elderly man shuts the heavy oak door behind him.

"So, Mike," he says, "how was the Sturgis Rally?"

"Fine," Mike replies. "It was a little rougher bunch than I'm used to, but I got along just fine. A good once-in-a-lifetime experience."

"Well, Mike, how long have you and Mary been married now – about five years – six?"

"Nearly seven, time flies," Mike replies.

"And, remember when you married my daughter, I said if you came to work for me – with me – that maybe one day this business would be yours?"

"Yes, I recall your saying that, Ed," Mike replies.

"Well, something came up that might make that a possibility a lot sooner than I had originally planned," Ed says.

"Really?" Mike replies with a big smile on his face.

Ed looks down before continuing. "But, there's a hitch," he says.

"What would that be?" Mike asks.

"Remember the Paxton County road construction project?" Ed asks.

"Sure, it was one of the biggest jobs the company ever had. Our biggest money maker ever, as I recall," Mike says.

"Well, that's where the hitch is," Ed says. "There's no good way to say this, so I'll just say it. The DCI was here for two days while you were away at Sturgis."

"The DCI?" Mike says.

"Department of Criminal Investigation," Ed replies. "They have been investigating the Paxton road job."

"Investigating? For what?" Mike says.

"Price fixing," Ed replies.

"Price fixing! Where did they get a crazy idea like that?" Mike asks.

Ed hangs his head, closes his eyes, and mutters, "It's true."

"How could that be?" Mike asks in shock.

"You know we've always been fierce competitors with Henderson Road Construction Company – well, we haven't always been as fierce competitors as Bill Henderson and I let on. There were two big road construction jobs back a couple of years ago – Paxton County and Winfield County. Well, Bill and I made a secret agreement that we'd fix the bids so he got Winfield and we got Paxton."

"I can't believe it," Mike says.

"It's done all the time, it's just that we got caught," Ed says. "They've got us; there's no way out."

"So, what's going to happen?" Mike asks, his face about as white as a sheet of typing paper by now.

"Somebody's going to jail," Ed says with a quivering voice.

"Somebody?" Mike asks, "Who are they looking at?"

"Me," Ed says, "they're looking at me," and then he breaks down sobbing.

Finally, Ed stops sobbing and dries his eyes. "But, I'm sixty-four years old and I can't go to jail. My heart's bad; I'd die in there."

"So, what are you going to do?" Mike asks.

"We, Mike, We. What are we going to do?" Ed says.

"What do you mean, *We?*" Mike asks slowly. "I had nothing to do with this – I knew nothing about it."

"That's what I'm coming to – they don't care who goes to jail, just as long as somebody goes," Ed says.

"What are you saying, Ed, what are you saying?" Mike says.

"I'll lay it out for you," Ed says. "I can't do jail time, but you're young and strong. They're only talking three years in one of those gentlemen federal prisons – Radios, TV's, libraries, workout rooms, good food, telephone use, no violent criminals – all white collar crime like us."

Mike is stunned. "So that's the deal – you want me to serve your prison sentence for you. You've always said I was like a son to you. This is how you treat your son?"

"I know, I know," Ed replies. "But, listen to the rest of the deal before you decide. If you do this for me, when you get out, which should be in three years, I'll sign the business over to you – it will be yours. You'll be a rich man."

Mike is stunned. "Mary would never go for it, not in a million years."

"We already talked about it," Ed replies. "She has agreed that it's the best way."

"My wife wants me to go to prison?" Mike says.

"Think of your kids," Ed says. "You will be able to raise them in style."

"I'll be a felon – a convict. Their dad will be a jailbird," Mike says.

"It'll blow over," Ed says. "You can do this."

Mike hangs his head and stares off into space.

"How much is the business worth?" Mike asks.

"Five million, give or take a few hundred thousand," Ed says.

"And you'd run the business while I'm away?" Mike says.

"I'll take good care of the business and it will be bigger and better than ever when you get out," Ed says.

"I'll have to talk to Mary to see if this is really what she wants, and if it is, I'll do it – but there are two conditions."

"Anything, I'll do anything," Ed says.

"You put one million dollars in an account with my name on it now and we go to a lawyer and draw up a contract for the transfer of the business the day after I get out," Mike demanded.

"Done," Ed says.

"I need to go talk to Mary," Mike says as he heads for

the door.

I have one serious question: when Mike goes to jail, will he have his billfold, and me, in his pocket, and will I spend three years in prison just like Mike? I had nothing to do with this, you know. I wasn't even minted when it happened.

ooooo

Mike gets in his car, drives about three miles to a public park that is nearly deserted, and parks his car.

He sits there for a moment, gathering his thoughts, and then he starts pounding the steering wheel and screaming.

Mike stops screaming and pounding and a sly smile comes over his face. "In less than a week I'll be a millionaire and in three years I'll be filthy rich – and the best part is I don't have to put up with that damn Ed's bragging and blowing, and bossing me around like I'm a teenager for the next three years. The other good part is, Ed doesn't know that it was me who proposed the Paxton-Winfield idea to Bill Henderson and that I was the guy who tipped off the DCI. Take that, Ed."

Mike wipes the smile off his face and heads home to talk to his wife.

Mystery Woman

Fortunately for me, Mike-the-Criminal left his billfold, containing me in the coin compartment, in the top drawer of his bedroom dresser when he went off to the gentlemen's prison. His father-in-law, Ed, drove him to the county jail, where the DCI agents were to take over.

Before Ed and Mike are even out of the driveway, Mary loots Mike's billfold and takes every penny he has, including me. A day later, Mary takes the kids to the candy store at the mall and I end up in the candy store's cash register.

A short time later, a short, rotund man with chubby cheeks comes in and buys a pound of chocolate covered cashews, and I am given to him in change.

Chubby Cheeks wanders around the mall for a couple of hours, nibbling on the chocolate covered cashews until they are gone. Then, he catches a cab to the airport and hops a plane to Atlanta, Georgia – home of peaches, country boys, and southern belles.

Chubby Cheeks stops at a gift shop on the concourse at the airport in Atlanta and buys a pound of chocolate covered peanuts. He scrounges around in his wallet and pockets until he finally comes up with the exact amount of the purchase price, $5.01. Of course, I am the $.01 and I am now in the store's cash register.

I am glad to get away from Chubby Cheeks before he explodes.

∞∞∞

Atlanta is hot, humid, and sticky, but stuff like that doesn't bother me a bit. What I don't like is being dropped in a bottle of Coke to see if I'll actually dissolve and I don't like having syrup spilled on me, either.

A woman walks into the gift shop and buys two gossip magazines and I am given to her in change. She is tall, slender, and plain. She has a librarian's face and wears little or no makeup. Her hair could use some work and her wardrobe could use a little updating. She's only thirty-five or forty and doesn't have a wedding ring. She probably never had a date in high school and went to a movie alone on prom night. But, she seems normal, sane, and happy, so she will be a nice change of pace from Mookey, Biker Babe, Mike-the-Crook, Chubby Cheeks, and the rest of them.

Librarian Face deposits me in her small leather purse and throws the long strap over her head and around her shoulder. The purse hangs by her side – no hands – practical. I'm not surprised – most librarians are practical.

I may have misjudged Librarian Face. We get to her car and it's a Mercedes two-seat convertible. Totally out of character, it seems to me. She is beginning to be intriguing.

An hour later, we arrive at Librarian Face's home on the outskirts of Atlanta. It is a brick house with white shutters and four white pillars extending from the ground to the second floor balcony—something like a modern-day Antebellum.

How would a woman like that afford something like this? A rich father, mother, or uncle? Maybe. A rich former husband? Naw. Won the lottery? Could happen. Earned it on her own? Hmmm.

ooooo

I have been in Librarian Face's purse for over three months and have been with her every second of every day. Her daily routine is puzzling, unusual, odd, and just plain weird. She starts the day by having breakfast at home and then promptly at 9:00 we arrive at a popular coffee shop, *Hey! Good Cookies!*

She orders a latte and chooses a small table close to a group of four to six women. Librarian Face breaks out a book and pretends to read, but she is really eavesdropping on the group of women.

After an hour of eavesdropping, Librarian Face goes to either the Atlanta Courthouse or the Fulton County Courthouse where she pours over public records.

Shortly before noon, she goes to a restaurant/bar near the courthouse, where she grabs a small table, orders a soda and a salad, and breaks out her book. Again, she pretends to be reading, but she's eavesdropping on the lawyers who grab a quick lunch and a cocktail or two before going back to court. Nosy. She is a very snoopy person.

After lunch, she goes back to the courthouse, and she

sits in on a trial that is in progress. It might be a murder trial, burglary trial, divorce hearing, or traffic ticket hearing – it doesn't seem to matter to her.

Once in a while, she skips going to the courthouse and spends the entire day at a nearby public library scanning newspapers from all over the country.

Whether she has been to the courthouse or the library, she returns home around 5:30 p.m. She turns on the television to a news channel while she fixes herself a small dinner. Then, she disappears upstairs.

If you think the stuff she does during the day is strange, get this: promptly at 7:00 p.m., she slowly comes down the winding staircase wearing silk pajamas. Some evenings the pajamas are yellow, sometimes red, blue, or black. If the pajamas are yellow, she normally wears glasses with round black rims, her hair is straight, and she bops down the steps as though walking on air. If the pajamas are red, her hair is all messed up and she has a glass of red wine in her hand as she slinks down the staircase. If the pajamas are blue, she descends the staircase with an aura of elegance. If the pajamas are black, her face is sullen and every step seems painful as she slowly descends into the depths of a personal darkness.

When she reaches the bottom of the staircase, she turns left and walks to a room that always has its door closed, day and night. She enters the room and closes the door behind her. I have never been in the room because I am in her purse and the purse is always placed in the same spot on a small entry table by the front door.

Night after night, I hear sounds coming from that room. When she wears the yellow pajamas, I sometimes hear her laughing. When she wears red pajamas, there is often loud Rock and Roll music from the 60's and 70's blaring and I can hear her yelling from time to time. When she wears blue pajamas, there is normally soft, elegant chamber music featuring lots of violins and I don't hear a sound out of Librarian Face. But, when she wears the black pajamas—when she wears black pajamas, strange things happen. There is loud symphony music with lots of tympani rolls, cymbal crashes, and passages that rise to a mighty crescendo. But, above all that, I can still hear what sounds like fists pounding on a desk or on the walls. And, there is moaning. She is moaning and groaning and I think she is crying. I wish I could go in there and comfort her.

Promptly at midnight, the door opens and Librarian Face walks out. Regardless of what color pajamas she is wearing or what seems to have gone on in that room, when she comes out, she is back to being totally normal. She seems content and pleased with herself. She climbs the staircase humming to herself and I don't see her again until 7:00 a.m., when the whole thing starts all over again.

The only difference in her weekly routine occurs on Sundays, when she goes into that room wearing her normal street clothes. She spends about two hours in there, without any music, laughing, screaming, pounding of fists, or crying. She comes out with a white shopping bag that appears to have something in the bottom of the bag. On Sunday night, she bakes a pan of cookies – sometimes chocolate chip, sometimes snicker doodle, sometimes sugar cookies with thick white or chocolate fudge frosting. After the cookies cool down, she places about a dozen of them in a covered dish and places the dish in the shopping bag. After that, she sinks into her favorite chair and reads two or three gossip magazines before going to bed.

On Monday morning, before going to *Hey! Good Cookies!* to eavesdrop on the groups of women, Librarian Face drops off the shopping bag at the apartment of a middle-aged woman who lives on Peachtree Street. The woman praises Librarian Face for last week's cookies, thanks her for the new batch, and returns the shopping bag and covered dish from last week's cookies. Something else might be in the bag, but I'm not sure. Then, we're quickly on our way. Another strange event in the life of Librarian Face.

Sure, I have tried to figure out what all of Librarian Face's strange, mysterious behavior means, but I really haven't been able to pin it down. Oh, I have some ideas, but they're just guesses. I think she might be a private detective or a spy for a foreign government. Maybe she is training to be a lawyer. Perhaps it is more simple than any of that: she is rich, bored, and weird and she does all of this strange stuff to simply kill time.

Well, you know as much about it as I do—what do you think?

ooooo

I probably never would have figured out what Librarian Face was up to if not for a sequence of events that occurred this morning – it's a Monday. Librarian face has eaten her breakfast and washed the dishes. She throws the strap of her purse, containing me in the coin compartment, over her head and shoulder, grabs the shopping bag containing the cookies, and is nearly to the front door when the phone rings.

She exchanges pleasant greetings with the caller and then says, "How many? Well, I'm really not sure – hang on while I go check."

Librarian Face heads straight to that secret room where she spends all of that time in her pajamas, and I am with her right there in her purse. She opens the door and flips on the light switch and what I see makes me flip.

The far wall is covered by a magnificent oak bookcase that is filled with reference books, décor, plaques, and mementos. A globe of the world that is inlaid with pearl and other precious stones occupies one shelf and a vintage Smith typewriter with round black keys sits on another. One shelf holds a collection of musical instruments including a large tambourine, a couple of maracas, and some castanets. One shelf holds two autographed footballs and an autographed basketball. There is a magnificent brass unicorn well over a foot tall on another shelf. Over in the corner, a Martin acoustic guitar rests on a holder. Hard to draw much of a conclusion about what is going on from this mishmash of stuff.

In front of the bookcase is a large wooden desk with

a soft leather chair behind it. A stack of typing paper about two inches thick, with double spaced typing visible on the top sheet, rests on one corner of the desk. A small stack of typing paper with handwriting visible occupies another corner of the desk. Two blue ink pens and two red ink pens rest on the desk top. A top-of-the-line sound system sits on a cabinet to the left of the desk.

All of this is pretty normal stuff for a home office, but what hangs on the walls is what makes this room so extraordinarily special. In an instant, the wall hangings reveal the final piece of the puzzle and I understand everything – the eavesdropping, courthouse research and trials, gossip magazines, trips to the library, dropping off of the shopping bag to the woman on Peachtree street, the Mercedes, the mansion. I know it all.

Librarian Face looks at the typed page on the top of the stack and we exit the secret room. She goes back to the phone in the kitchen and says, "five hundred seventeen." She exchanges a few more pleasantries with the caller, grabs the shopping bag, and we head for Peachtree street and the rest of our Monday routine.

Librarian Face switches it up a bit at *Hey! Good Cookies!* and orders a cup of black coffee and a Scotcheroo. The total comes to $6.26 and she reaches in her purse and grabs a $5, a $1, a quarter—and to my horror – me - to pay the tab.

I am sad to part ways with Librarian Face, but if she had ordered the coffee and Scotcheroo just one day sooner, I never would have learned what I now know.

ooooo

I am lying here in the cash register at *Hey! Good Cookies!* reminiscing about the past thirteen or fourteen weeks as Librarian Face's constant companion in her purse. I also reflect on how easy it is to get the wrong impression or image of a person based on their hair style, clothing, or looks.

When I first met Librarian Face, I saw a tall, slender, plain-looking woman with an old-fashioned hair style and clothes that were out of date. Little did I know at the time that this was all an act to not draw attention to the real person beneath that disguise.

I discovered the real Librarian Face during our time together, and she is a warm, kind, talented, beautiful, hard-working person.

In the few seconds that I was in her secret office this morning, I also discovered from the more than one hundred framed book covers lining her walls that she is *Blaize Cameron* – the most successful and most famous romance writer that has ever lived. She is famous not only for turning out a dozen page-turners a year, but for creating books that are real and authentic. You can thank her eavesdropping and courthouse and library research—and probably her yellow, red, blue, and black silk pajamas for that.

Blaize Cameron is also famous for not wanting to be famous. As far as I know, there are only two people on earth who know that Librarian Face is actually Blaize Cameron –

her agent who called this morning and her typist on Peachtree street. And then, there's me, but like one of Blaize Cameron's characters in one of her books, I vow to keep her secret until eternity or until they melt me down.

"Farewell, Blaize, my love. It was not our fate to spend forever together, but I will never forget you."

(What do you think — do I have a future as a romance writer?)

Hallelujah!

For nearly two months after I was dropped into the cash register at *Hey! Good Cookies!* I circulated around Atlanta and the surrounding area. I passed through the hands of retail clerks, waitresses, lawyers, doctors, factory workers, nurses, postal workers, government workers, teachers, cab drivers, police officers, truck drivers, a hooker, and a very unusual and memorable preacher, Rev. H. R. Brown.

I met Rev. H.R. Brown in a bar in a seedy part of Atlanta when he bought a bag of peanuts and asked the bartender if he could get a few pennies and nickels as part of his change, which included me. Rev. H.R. Brown wasn't in the bar drinking – he was there to save souls as part of what he called his "Bar Crawl Ministry."

One day every week, the Good Reverend hangs out in a dive or tavern for an hour or two and casually chats with some of Atlanta's finest drinkers. He doesn't lay a heavy dose of religion or guilt on the boozers – he just offers encouragement and assistance if they need it and he offers a simple message, "God loves you." His philosophy is that he can have a more powerful impact on these people by living his faith than by preaching about it.

After leaving Lefty's Sports Bar, Rev. H.R. Brown went straight to his office at his church. He removed the change he got from the bartender, five pennies, including me, and four nickels, and placed us in a paper cup on the corner of his desk. He then set about working on his sermon for next Sunday.

ooooo

It is Sunday. I, along with the other change, have been in the cup on Rev. H.R. Brown's desk for three days and it appears he may have forgotten about us.

At twenty minutes before nine o'clock, Rev. H.R. Brown enters his office, pours all of us out of the cup into his hand and puts us in his pants pocket. And, what a pants pocket it is!

The Reverend H.R. Brown looks downright splendid! He is wearing a yellow suit with a purple necktie. His yellow patent leather shoes match the shade of his suit and they shine almost as much as me. He's wearing a yellow hat with a white hatband. Of course, the yellow hat matches his suit and shoes. The final touch is a diamond ring half the size of Rhode Island on the little finger of his left hand.

The Good Reverend admires his appearance in the full length mirror, gives himself a wink, and it's time to go. Show Time!

The Rev. H.R. Brown enters the chapel at the front of the church through a side door, which is the cue for the choir to kick off the first song. There are at least thirty of them in the choir, all in flowing blue robes. The piano accompanist plays an old upright and she has it rocking as the choir launches into a rousing version of "Mighty Clouds of Joy."

Members of the congregation are dressed every bit as fine as The Reverend. Women are wearing heels and brightly colored dresses, many of which are floor length. All of the men wear suits, many of which are snazzy red, blue, white, yellow, or green. Most of the men and all of the women wear hats. Even the children are finely dressed.

The congregation is on their feet, clapping their hands, rocking to the music and singing along. The spirit of the music has grabbed Rev. H.R. Brown and he cannot contain himself as he displays a few dance moves that could have landed him a spot on American Bandstand. The other coins and I in his pocket are bouncing up and down as The Good Reverend busts a few moves.

Rev. H.R. Brown addresses the choir after their first song, "That's righteous," he says, "real righteous."

The rockin' piano player and the choir launch into another toe-tapper, "Oh, Happy Day," which is well received by the congregation. Now, it is time for a few words from Rev. H.R. Brown.

"People, People," he says, "we have done things that we should not have done."

Members of the congregation nod their heads in agreement and several shout, "Amen."

Rev. H.R. Brown continues, "People, we have not done things that we should have done."

Again members of the congregation nod their heads in agreement and several shout, "Amen."

"People, we have to do better," The Good Reverend says.

Members of the congregation nod their heads in agreement and several shout "Amen," and "Hallelujah."

And that's it – twenty-nine words, the sermon is over, and the choir swings into a sweet version of, "Swing Low, Sweet Chariot."

Rev. H.R. Brown says, "It is now time for our offering to keep this fine church operating and to do the Lord's work. Give generously. And, for you children," he says as he walks over to a plastic replica of the church building and removes its roof, "we have the *Noisy Offering*. Come up here and drop your pennies, nickels, dimes, and quarters into the *Noisy Offering* like this . . ."

With that, Rev. H.R. Brown reaches into his pocket and withdraws me and the other coins that had been in the cup on his desk and he throws us into the plastic church. As we bounce off the plastic walls, we create one heck of a racket – definitely a *Noisy Offering*.

Kids beg for coins from their parents and charge up to throw their coins into the plastic church to make as much noise as they can. You have to admire Rev. H.R. Brown for devising a way to train kids to be good givers from an early age.

The choir sings one more song, "The Unclouded Day," and the service is over.

Halfway through the final chorus of "The Unclouded Day," the Rev. H.R. Brown leaves the church to position himself on the front steps to greet each parishioner as they leave the church.

I never saw Rev. H.R. Brown again, but I'll say one thing—his church service was a lot more fun than one of Mookey's Rock and Roll concerts, and that's saying something. Hallelujah!

A Wedding to Remember

I, along with the other coins in the *Noisy Offering* and the money from the offering plates spent the night in the safe in Rev. H.R. Brown's office. Monday morning, the church treasurer takes us to Atlanta National Bank and Trust Company and deposits us. I, along with the other coins are put in the cash drawer by a pretty, middle-aged woman. There are only a few other pennies in here, so we have plenty of room. That is, until the cashier breaks open a roll of freshly-minted pennies and dumps them in on top of the rest of us.

I don't want to be arrogant or sound like an elitist, but I really don't like associating with those puny new pennies made of 97.5% zinc and only 2.5% copper. In case you have forgotten, I am 95% copper—I am the real deal and those new pennies are pathetic imitations.

I have been in the cash drawer, commingled with those puny pennies of lesser value, for over two hours. Every time the cashier reaches into the drawer to grab a penny or two I pray it will be me and I can get away from these dreadful zinc pennies.

Finally, around noon, it happens. A pretty woman in her mid twenties comes in with her monthly paycheck of $855.27. Her name is Marcy. She explains that she is heading to Nashville for the bachelorette party and wedding of one of her former college roommates. She deposits $600 in her checking account and takes the rest, $255.27, in cash. She stuffs the money, including me, into her purse and we are on our way.

The drive from Atlanta to downtown Nashville takes a little over five hours. It would have been faster if she wouldn't have had to stop for gas twice and for a quart of oil two more times for her gas guzzlin', oil-burning, smokin' 1977 Chevy Chevelle.

Marcy enters the DoubleTree Hotel in downtown Nashville and is met in the lobby by three screaming women that she apparently hasn't seen for quite a while. They will sleep two to a room in adjoining rooms.

After they check in, they walk a couple of blocks to Tootsie's Orchid Lounge on Lower Broadway. It is across the alley from the Ryman Auditorium, former home of the famous Grand Ole Opry. Tootsie's was a famous watering hole for many Grand Ole Opry stars who would have a few drinks and listen to the Opry on the radio until they were announced as the next performer. Then they would run across the alley and charge onto the stage just in time to do their show.

Marcy and the other three young ladies walk into Tootsie's and are met with screams from the bride-to-be, Samantha, and three other women. The eight of them crowd around a corner table and order straight shots of Tequila. After two rounds, the party is in full swing and they sing along with the band to the Judds' "Why Not Me?" with gusto.

Marcy is the self-appointed photographer for this rolling party and is on her second roll of film before they even leave Tootsie's.

The bachelorette party picks up steam as they wander from one honkytonk to another up and down Lower Broadway.

Around ten o'clock, the bachelorette party comes face to face with the bachelor party, which is also carousing Lower Broadway. The groom-to-be, Adrian, is proud of his ability to hold his liquor and vows to party until they throw him and his entourage out at closing time.

Only a few of the bridesmaids and groomsmen knew each other before this night and the rest of them get acquainted fast. The two groups splinter, with some of the men and women going off together and some of them sticking with their original groups. Samantha and Adrian decide they will have the rest of their lives together, so tonight they will party with their friends instead of hanging out together.

ooooo

The plan was simple—the bachelorette and bachelor parties would be on Wednesday night. Thursday would be a day of shopping for the women and golf for the guys. Friday was a free day to do whatever came along and Friday night would be the wedding rehearsal and the rehearsal dinner. The wedding was scheduled for Saturday at 3:00 p.m.

It is Thursday morning and the bachelorettes are in varying degrees of recovery from the night before. Several, including Samantha and Marcy, turned in shortly after midnight and are in a festive mood this morning. Several closed down the bars at 2:00 a.m. and a couple, including the Maid of Honor, Lisa, rolled in around 4:00 a.m. after finding a private party at a suite in the Sheraton Hotel a couple of blocks away. They will sleep in for a while.

Samantha, Marcy, and two of the other bridesmaids eat a quick breakfast in the DoubleTree Cafe and head directly to the newly remodeled Mall at Green Hills, one of the mid-south's premier shopping destinations. They locate a One-Hour Photo shop and drop off the seven rolls of film that were shot by Marcy, and later by others from the group when Marcy went back to the hotel around midnight.

A couple of hours later, Samantha and Marcy pick up the developed photos and find a corner table in the food court where they eagerly go through them. Some are funny, some are goofy, some are outrageous, some are boring, some are hilarious. Some of the photos taken by others after Marcy turned in for the night are surprising, shocking, and downright scandalous. Other photos, if they got out, might end careers or even put someone in jail. Samantha and Marcy discuss at length which photos to share with the others and which would be best ripped to shreds and deposited in the trash never to be seen by another set of human eyes. Ultimately, since Samantha is the bride-to-be and it is her show, they decided it is her decision to make. A few go into the trash.

ooooo

Friday's rehearsal goes well, except for finding enough room at the alter for the bride, groom, and seven bridesmaids and seven groomsmen. By now, everyone in the wedding party is well acquainted and the rehearsal resembles a party, albeit a rather sober party.

The rehearsal dinner, held at one of Nashville's finest restaurants, Dominique's, is somewhat of a low key affair, since the bride's and groom's rather conservative families are in attendance and dampen the frivolity.

The groom-to-be, Adrian, is in his normal upbeat, wisecracking, cavalier mood. Samantha, however, looks like the relentless pace of the past three days is taking its toll and maybe there is a little pre-wedding jitters.

After the rehearsal, some of the wedding party go out on the town, promising to not overdo it so they will be in good shape for tomorrow's wedding.

Marcy and Samantha go to the Steel Guitar and Fiddle Bar in Printer's Alley, a couple of blocks from Lower Broadway. It's early and the place is not crowded – they take a table in the back of the room. They slowly sip on two margaritas while they engage in a deep, serious conversation.

I have been in Marcy's purse ever since she left Atlanta, so I have seen and heard just about everything that she has. There is something else afoot, though, that I was not previously aware of, but I'm starting to get an inkling of what it's about.

ooooo

It is Saturday afternoon, and the atmosphere surrounding the bride-to-be and her seven attendants is electric.

Marcy goes to Samantha's room, where she has just gotten into her wedding gown. Marcy asks the two other women in the room with Samantha if they can have a moment alone and they graciously leave the room.

It is the biggest day of Samantha's life and although she is excited, she also seems calm, collected, and confident.

"Are you going through with it?" Marcy asks.

"Yes," Samantha says resolutely, "in fact, I am really looking forward to it."

Marcy reaches into her purse and grabs me. "Here," she says to Samantha, "put this penny in your shoe for luck."

Samantha takes me and slips me into her right shoe.

Samantha and Marcy hug and Marcy leaves the room.

I'm going to be in a wedding!

∞∞∞

Two vans come to the DoubleTree to transport Samantha, the seven bridesmaids, and me to the church. We arrive twenty minutes before the ceremony is to begin.

∞∞∞

I do not have other weddings to judge this one by, but I would say it was a wonderful wedding and it went off without a hitch. The bride was beautiful, and the seven bridesmaids looked radiant. The groom and groomsmen all had a rosy glow to their cheeks, which probably means they had been drinking in the church basement before the ceremony, but at least none of them passed out at the altar.

ooooo

We are now at Dominique's banquet room for the wedding dinner. Five long tables stretch across the front of the room where the bride, groom, and fourteen attendants are seated.

More than two hundred invited guests are seated at tables covered with linen tablecloths and champagne is flowing freely. Guests have a dinner choice of Steak Oscar with Hollandaise sauce and fresh asparagus, jumbo prawns with Boston Browns, or spaghetti.

After everyone has been served, the best man rises to propose a toast to the newlyweds. He raises his champagne glass, takes a gulp, and begins, "Adrian and I met when we were freshmen in college and we have been best friends ever since. Back when we were freshmen, our lives revolved around how much beer we could drink and how many women we could get into the sack. As time went on, though, Adrian became more polished and sophisticated and switched to drinking brandy and then tequila until he finally developed a taste for fine Kentucky bourbon.

"His taste in women improved, too, and by the time we

were seniors, he was dating the homecoming queen and the daughter of the University's Chancellor. Wow! And, then, just when I thought he had reached the pinnacle of his dating career, he met Samantha. I can honestly say that Samantha and Adrian are soul mates. She is the only woman that he ever dated that can keep up with him drinking, and swearing, and, well—in other ways, too, if you get what I mean. So, I'd like to wish Adrian and Samantha a long and happy life together. Cheers!"

Maybe it was the champagne or maybe it is because the best man is an idiot, but that was a speech that most people in attendance will not soon forget.

Lisa, the Maid of Honor, is next to make a toast to the newlyweds. She praises Samantha for being such a wonderful and loyal friend for the past ten years, since they first met in high school. She wishes the newlyweds a happy life together, and that is it. Short and sweet.

Next, Adrian rises to make a short speech, in which he thanks everyone for coming and praises Samantha's parents for providing "one of the best meals I ever had in my life." Before he sits down, he raises his glass toward Samantha and makes a toast, "To Samantha, my wonderful wife. I pledge to you my undying, total, and complete love and faithfulness for the rest of our lives." It is almost enough to bring a tear to a glass eye.

Now it is Samantha's turn. "Thank all of you for coming to this very special event. I hope you enjoyed the wonderful meal and the delicious champagne. This is a day that I will always remember, and perhaps you will always remember it as well. I would especially like to thank all of my wonderful friends who were my bridesmaids. Some of you have not had a chance to meet them, so I'd like to introduce them to you and tell you a little bit about each of them. I have prepared a short slide presentation."

One of the waiters had set up a slide projector so it would show images against the wall to the right of the head table. Samantha holds the projector's control in her hand and pushes the button to show the first slide. In turn, Samantha flips through a photo of each of her attendants, which had been taken before they went honkytonkin' Wednesday night. There was Diane, Kim, Beverly, Karissa, Marilyn, Marcy, and lastly, Lisa, her Maid of Honor.

Next, Samantha flips through a few fun slides from the bachelorette party, none of which were too revealing or too scandalous.

Samantha pushes the button and an image of a scantily-clothed Lisa, hugging Adrian, lights up the wall and she says, "Here is my Maid of Honor, Lisa, hugging my fiancee' Wednesday night." Samantha shoots a dagger at Lisa, who is suddenly as white as a ghost.

Lisa shields her mouth from the crowd with her hand and mouths the word, "Don't." She begs, "Please Don't."

And then, Samantha pushes the button again and the crowd gasps. "And, this is my fiancee screwing my Maid of Honor."

Samantha takes off her right shoe, the one that I am in,

and throws it at her husband, "You cheating son-of-a-bitch," she yells.

I fly out of her shoe and land in a bridesmaid's plate of spaghetti.

Samantha takes off her other shoe and throws it at Lisa, "You backstabbing bitch," she screams.

Everyone is too stunned to move or to say anything.

"I'm outta here," Samantha yells as she heads for the door. Marcy jumps up to follow her and the rest of the bridesmaids follow suit, leaving Lisa sitting there to deal with the aftermath.

This was my first wedding reception, so I don't have any others to compare it to, but I'm going to give it an A+++ for originality, excitement, showmanship, and memorability. I had a hunch that something like this might happen, because I heard Samantha and Marcy discussing it last night at the Steel Guitar and Fiddle Bar, but I really didn't think Samantha would do it. But, pull it off she did, and as she had said at the beginning of her speech, this was a day she would never forget, and that the guests would not forget either. No shit.

I already told you that I do not like being dropped into a bottle of Coke to see if I will dissolve and I don't like having syrup spilled on me. Add this to that list: I don't like being in a plate of spaghetti, either.

Tootsie's Revisited

Within moments of Samantha's departure, followed by her bridesmaids, the stunned dinner guests quietly leave the banquet room. Finally, Adrian gets up to leave. He stops next to Lisa, who is sobbing uncontrollably. "I'm sorry," he says softly. "I'm going to go find Samantha and see if I can fix this."

"You got me drunk and took advantage of me," Lisa says through sobs.

Adrian slowly walks out of the banquet room staring at the floor, followed by his groomsmen. The last one, Ken, stops and puts his hand on Lisa's shoulder. "Come," he says gently. "I'll give you a ride."

The waiters and waitresses, most of whom have witnessed the entire thing, respectfully wait until everyone has left before they start clearing tables.

I am lying here in this half-eaten bowl of spaghetti, contemplating my future. In a few minutes this plate and I will be carried into the kitchen and somebody will probably run me down an industrial strength garbage disposal that will chew me into little pieces and wash me down the drain and into the sewer system. Another possibility is that the spaghetti and I will be dumped into the plastic liner of a garbage can that will be thrown into a dumpster later tonight and hauled off to the landfill in the morning.

What a choice—spending eternity in the sewer or in the dump.

The waiter stacks ten plates on top of me, carries me into the kitchen, and stacks me on a table next to a guy who is dumping leftovers into the garbage can and washing dishes by hand. Well, at least my beautiful shine and gorgeous copper body won't get ground to bits by a garbage disposal.

Dishwasher Guy holds my plate in his left hand and has a spatula in his right hand, ready to send me into oblivion. He glances down at the plate of spaghetti and says, "Well, lookit here. Look what I found." He reaches into that plate and pulls me from the gooey mess.

Dishwasher Guy washes me off and dries me with a dish towel. He admires me. "What a nice, shiny penny. I'll bet some waiter gave somebody crappy service and they tipped the waiter a penny to get even – and they threw the penny in this bowl of spaghetti. Yup, that's probably what happened."

And with that said, Dishwasher Guy puts me in his right front pants pocket where I come to rest among a bunch of odd-shaped pieces of plastic.

"Tonight's my last night," Diswasher Guy says to the chef, "I'm quitting."

"What are you going to do for a job when you leave here?" the chef asks.

"I got a gig down at Tootsie's, playing three hours an afternoon with some guys in a band we put together. We been practicin' and we're pretty damn good. Come down and listen to us, three o'clock tomorrow afternoon."

∞∞∞

A band is on stage, right inside Tootsie's front door, when Dishwasher Guy and his group show up with their equipment a few minutes before three o'clock. The band on stage finishes its final song and tears down its equipment in about five minutes. They empty a wad of cash from a gallon pickle jar sitting on the corner of the stage and they are out of there.

Dishwasher Guy, who's name is Randy, I find out, and the rest of his band set up in about five minutes and are ready to go.

They launch into their first song, "That's the Way Love Goes," and Randy wasn't bragging—they sound damn good. Randy plays rhythm guitar and is the lead singer. He has a rich deep baritone voice that is unique, soft, and powerful, all at the same time.

Randy's band plays a combination of current country hits like "Somebody's Gonna Love You," "Smokey Mountain Rain," and "I Guess it Never Hurts to Hurt Sometimes," along with some Hank Williams classics like "Your Cheatin' Heart," and "Kaw-Liga."

About every fifteen minutes, Randy recruits a good-looking, upbeat woman to grab the pickle jar to go from table to table for tips. As Randy announces each time, "The band only plays for tips, so we appreciate whatever you can give."

Everyone throws in a buck or two and some drop a $5 or $10 into the jar. It looks like Randy found a better paying job than dishwashing.

The band is hot and the bar is packed from wall to wall, with people standing in line outside waiting to get in. Every now and then, Randy throws his plastic guitar pick to some lovely lady or drunk in the crowd, which is sure to increase tips. He reaches into his right front pants pocket and fishes out another pick for the next song.

After flipping a half dozen picks into the crowd, Randy reaches into his pocket and the only thing in there is me. He grabs me and uses me for a pick for the next song.

How many pennies can say they played in a hot country band in Tootsie's on Lower Broadway in Nashville! Yee Haw!!

After using me for a pick for two songs, Randy flips me into the crowd and I am grabbed by a middle-aged man with unruly curly hair, a thick mustache, and wire-rimmed glasses. He carefully tucks me into his wallet as a souvenir from Tootsie's, and from Randy and the band.

Whoda Thunk It - Me Off to College

Curly Haired Mustachioed One left Nashville around five o'clock and drove straight through to Mobile, Alabama, arriving home at about 1 a.m. He flopped down on the couch, exhausted, and slept until 7 a.m., took a quick shower, got dressed, and headed to work.

Curly Haired One parks his car in the faculty parking lot at Kingman University, enters the building, and goes straight to his office. The name on the office door says, Harlan D. Moscowitz, Ph.D., Professor of Mathematics.

From the conversation among Professor Moscowitz's colleagues, it is apparent this is the first day of summer school classes. The summer session will last six weeks and a three credit course will meet for an hour and a half each day, five days a week.

ooooo

Today is Friday and there is only one week left in the summer session. I have been observing Professor Moscowitz over these past five weeks and here are my conclusions:

1. The Good Professor values his time, does not want to waste any of it and believes in what he calls *Precision*

Timing. That is, for his first class of the day, that starts at 9 a.m., he arrives in his office precisely at 8:55, grabs his textbook and lecture notes and charges down the hallway, arriving at his classroom at precisely 8:59:59.

2. Professor Moscowitz's desk is covered with a stack of books, papers, and magazines about one foot thick. To read or prepare for class, he sits on a folding chair in the corner of his office, directly beneath a picture of Albert Einstein.

3. For light reading in his spare time, Professor Moscowitz has been reading *The Behavioral Interaction Between Quantitative Analysis and Mathematical Psychology.* He often chuckles and sometimes laughs out loud when something tickles his fancy.

4. The Professor always wears a sport coat with leather elbow patches. He has at least eight of them.

5. Professor Moscowitz normally works with his office door closed, probably because he mutters to himself about his students, his colleagues, and the University administrators.

6. During class, Professor Moscowitz often becomes exasperated with his students and when he turns to write something on the board, he often mutters something to himself, such as, "Why me, Lord, why me?" "That's the dumbest answer I ever heard," "Lord, take me now," and "I should have been a truck driver."

Class is in session and Professor Moscowitz is at the board, listing the steps to the solution of the mathematical brainteaser that he assigned for today. He is on Step Eight when he sneaks a peek at his work and notices what he wrote down for Step Five. He mutters under his breath, "Oh shit."

Lightning fast, the Professor weighs his options. On one hand, he could say something like, "Class, in reviewing my work, I see that I made an error in Step Five, which will compound itself through all of the remaining steps in solving this problem. Let me go back and start over—and I hope I did not confuse you too badly."

Professor Moscowitz mutters to himself, "I'm in too deep to turn back now and I'm sure as hell not going to admit to this bunch of dumb shits that I'm capable of making an error. I'll give 'em a snow job that they'll never forget."

Professor Moscowitz continues to write feverishly on the board and when he is finished he explains his step-by-step calculations to the class.

"The inversion of the algorithm of the sine of number four divided by the congruent polynominal tangent of the number fourteen multiplied by the random variable of the number seven, when divided by the square root of zero, results in the permutation of the quadrilateral function of the sum of the subtrahend and the minuend divided by their inversion, added to the concentric isometry of the free radical number thirty-two, which results in, as you can readily see, the answer – *Three.*"

"Any Questions?"

ooooo

It is the final day of the summer session. Classes ended at 2 p.m. today and grades are due to be turned in by the faculty to the Registrar by 5 p.m. Professor Moscowitz has cleared off his desk, stacking everything against the wall, so he can get to work on calculating final grades.

The Professor grades on the total point basis, with the minimum number of points needed for a grade as follows:

A-245, B-215, C-170, D-140, F-below 140.

Professor Moscowitz is assigning grades: "Bill, 247 points, A; Linda, 182 points, C; Calvin, 216 points, but he has been a pain in the ass, so I'm going to deduct three points, C; Mary, 210 points, but she's got a nice smile and she always turns her work in on time, I'll add ten points, B; Timothy, 137 points, but he always came to class and was a good laugher when I told a joke; I'll add four points, D.

There is a light knock on Professor Moscowitz's door and he says, "Come in."

A timid, scared young woman enters the office and says, "Uh, I'm Jeanie Logan in your, uh, nine o'clock class, and I was wondering what I got for a final grade."

Professor Moscowitz scans his grade book and says, "I'm sorry, but you only had 116 points and a minimun of 140 is needed for a D.

"So, I failed the course?" Jeanie asks.

"I'm afraid that you did," the Professor says kindly, "but maybe you could take it again next summer session, which starts on Monday."

"I can't attend next summer session," she says, "I have a summer job lined up that starts on Monday."

"I'm sorry, I really am," Professor Moscowitz says.

Jeanie is not about to give up easily. She says, "I really liked the course, and I studied hard every day three or four hours, and I think you're a great teacher, but I just couldn't figure out all of those formulas.

"If I don't pass this course, I won't be able to graduate and my family will be so terribly disappointed in me and they are all coming to the graduation ceremony on Sunday and it will be terribly embarrassing for me if they come and I'm not in the ceremony.

"I know based on my test scores that I deserve an F, but I'll do extra credit if I can just raise it to a D minus."

And then Jeanie says, "But the main thing is, I just don't want to be a failure," and then she breaks down and cries.

Professor Moscowitz thinks for a moment, and then he spins his office chair around, puts a sheet of paper in his typewriter, and begins typing. When he is finished, he hands the sheet to Jeanie.

AGREEMENT

I, Jeanie Logan, do hereby admit that I am absolutely horrible at performing mathematical calculations. I also admit that I earned an "F" and deserved and "F" in the Mathematics course that I took. I hereby agree to the following, in return for having my final grade raised from the "F" that I deserved to a "D" in the Mathematics course.

I, Jeanie Logan, promise to never, ever, my entire life, even if I am threatened or beaten, divulge to anyone, either directly or indirectly, that I ever took a Mathematics course from Professor Harlan Moscowitz.

Signed: _____

Jeanie Logan

Jeanie reads the words on the paper very carefully and then looks at Professor Moscowitz with hopeful eyes. "Are you serious?" she asks.

"Yes, I am," he replies. "You agree to never, ever, the rest of your life, tell a soul that you took a Mathematics course from me and I'll give you a D."

Jeanie quickly signs the paper and gives it back to Professor Moscowitz before he has time to change his mind.

Professor Moscowitz records her final grade, "D" on his grade sheet and shows it to Jeanie.

Jeanie says, "Thank you, Thank you, Thank you."

Professor Moscowitz says, "You're welcome – now go on and have a good life."

Jeanie leaves his office walking on air, Professor Moscowitz allows himself a thin smile, and he goes back to work: "Angelena, 212 points, but she's got a great. . . ."

ooooo

The second summer session starts on Monday and Professor Moscowitz shows up at his normal time, 8:55, even though his first class does not start until 10:00.

He scans his class list for the new courses and suddenly starts muttering, "No, No, No! Not again! Not that damned Wilfred Fenney. Why me, Lord, why me?"

Professor Moscowitz is in a near panic, until an idea hits him. He wheels around, puts a sheet of paper in his typewriter and begins typing like a madman.

Professor Moscowitz addresses his 10:00 class with the normal first-day pleasantries, hands out the course outline, describes the course attendance policy, gives the class an assignment for the following day, and turns them loose.

"Wilfred," he says, "can I talk to you a minute."

"Sure, Professor Moscowitz—what's up?"

"Come to my office," the Professor says.

Wilfred follows Professor Moscowitz to his office and sits down across from the Professor's desk.

"Wilfred, you're a very pleasant fellow and a nice guy and personally, I like you," Professor Moscowitz says.

"Thanks, Professor," Wilfred says with a broad smile on his face.

"How many of my classes have you signed up for in the past, not including this one?" the Professor asks.

"Well, I guess that would be four classes," Wilfred says.

"And how many of them did you finish?" Moscowitz asks.

"Well, I, ah, had some difficulties and some personal

problems and some financial problems, and some issues and, ah . . . well, I didn't finish any of them," Wilfred confesses.

"Right," the Professor says. "Your normal M.O. is to show up for class the first day, miss four or five days in a row, show up a time or two, and disappear until the final day you can drop the course when you show up with your drop slip – that sound about right?"

Wilfred smiles sheepishly, "Ya, that's the way it normally goes."

"Well, Wilfred, it occurred to me that my normal class attendance policy and penalty for missing class is not a strong enough incentive for you to attend class, so I have devised a special attendance policy just for you."

Professor Moscowitz hands Wilfred the sheet he had typed just that morning.

AGREEMENT

This agreement is entered into between Professor Harlan D. Moscowitz, a Professor of Mathematics at Kingman University and hereinafter referred to as THE PROFESSOR and Wilfred Fenney, a student at Kingman University and hereinafer referred to as THE STUDENT.

WHEREAS THE PROFESSOR is instructor of the Mathematics course, hereinafter identified as THE COURSE, and THE STUDENT is enrolled in THE COURSE.

WHEREAS in the past the standard attendance policy for courses taught by THE PROFESSOR and taken by THE STUDENT have been highly ineffective in encouraging THE

STUDENT to attend classes.

THEREFORE, the following special attendance policy shall be in effect between THE PROFESSOR and THE STUDENT for THE COURSE.

THE PROFESSOR shall pay THE STUDENT the sum of TWO DOLLARS ($2.00) for each time that THE STUDENT attends a class session of THE COURSE.

THE STUDENT shall pay to THE PROFESSOR the sum of ONE DOLLAR ($1.00) for each time that THE STUDENT misses a class session of THE COURSE.

Final settlement of the amount owed between THE PROFESSOR and THE STUDENT shall be made on the day of the final exam for THE COURSE.

This document contains the full and complete agreement between THE PROFESSOR and THE STUDENT.

The signatures of the parties bind them to the terms of this agreement.

———————————————   ———————————————

Professor Moscowitz   *Wilfred Fenney*

Wilfred reads the agreement intently and then looks at Professor Moscowitz and smiles. "Are you serious?" he asks.

"Absolutely," the Professor says.

"How many times does the course meet during this summer session?" Wilfred asks.

"It meets five days a week for six weeks – thirty times," Professor Moscowotz replies.

"You'd pay me two dollars a class for thirty classes? That's uh . . ."

"Sixty dollars," Moscowitz says, "but remember, you will owe me a dollar for every class you miss. You could actually end up owing me money."

"No way," Wilfred says as he signs the document.

Professor Moscowitz fetches his wallet from his back pocket, opens the coin compartment, and grabs me. "Here," he says, handing me to Wilfred. "This is to bind the deal."

Wilfred smiles as he puts me in his pocket and leaves Professor Moscowitz's office.

Professor Moscowsitz scribbles a formula on a piece of paper and punches some numbers into his calculator. "Ahha!" he says with a satisfied smile on his face as he rubs his hands together, "There's a 89.74% chance I'll never see Wilfred Fenney again."

ooooo

Wilfred goes straight from Professor Moscowitz's office to The Tap Inn on twelfth street. "You still got those tap beers for a penny?" he asks.

"Yup, the first beer's a penny—after that, they're a buck," the bartender says.

Wilfred reaches in his pocket, grabs me, and flips me onto the bar. "This one's on Professor Harlan D. Moscowitz," he says with a broad grin.

"Machine Gun Moscowitz? I had him for class some

years ago. I dropped my pencil one time and missed two pages of lecture notes," the bartender says with a smile.

"That's him," Wilfred says.

"You taking a math class from Moscowitz this session?" the bartender asks as he serves Wilfred his beer.

"I was thinking about it, but I don't know if I can afford it. Maybe I'll take the course from someone else next fall," Wilfred says.

The bartender picks me up off of the bar, turns around and drops me into a metal box about a foot tall with the Jack Daniels emblem on it. The box is almost level full with pennies.

When the bartender turns around to see if Wilfred wants another beer, the glass is empty and Wilfred Fenney is gone.

Life at the Tap Inn

At first when Professor Moscowitz gave me to that knothead Wilfred Fenney, I was a little ticked off at him. I liked hanging around with The Professor. He was pretty funny, in a subtle way, especially when he muttered to himself about his students, saying stuff like, "Why me, Lord, why me?" or "Lord, take me now."

His students probably thought he was a hardass, but deep down, he really cares about them. Sure, he doctored a few student grades up or down a smidgen, but then, his grading scale permitted a small amount of mathematical deviation and in the end, everybody got the grade that they deserved.

It is now the middle of September and I have been in this metal can on the back of the bar in The Tap Inn for about two months. The bartender only dumped three additional pennies into the can before he proclaimed the can "full," and he broke out another can and started filling it.

The Tap Inn is a long, narrow bar with a stage just inside the front door, much like a lot of the honkytonks in Nashville. There is a dance floor in front of the stage. The bar along the wall to the right seats about fifteen people and there is room for another four people on each end of the bar. During the daytime, there is only one bartender, but there are two bartenders from four in the afternoon until closing time.

There are three pool tables in the back of the bar along with two dart boards. There are at least a dozen television sets that are positioned so no matter where you sit you can see the ball game that's on.

Above the bar is a stuffed moose head and below it is The Tap Inn's slogan, "A Saloon Without A Moose Is Just A Bar."

It is interesting watching the people who come into The Tap Inn. It is two in the afternoon. The couple sitting in the dark corner in the back—the 60-year-old man in the suit with the well-dressed 30-year-old woman who laughs hilariously at every dumb thing he says, is a businessman and his secretary who knocked off from work early. He's trying to get into her pants and she's trying to get into his wallet. As the guys sitting at the bar would say, "Tit for Tat."

At precisely 4:15 every afternoon, John shows up and sits in the second bar stool from the end of the bar, right in front of the beer spigots. The bartender, Mandy, sees him coming and has his penny beer on the bar before he even sits down. When John wants a refill, he slides his empty glass forward two inches and Mandy fills it within ten seconds. This continues for two hours until John has his nightly fill of a dozen tap beers.

There are at least thirty regulars who can be counted on every night of the week for an hour or two and the college crowd normally shows up around 10:00 p.m., already half in the bag.

Occasionally, a stranger shows up like the time a guy

wearing a suit and tie burst in through the back door, and yelled to the bartender, "Give me a shot of whiskey and a beer." He gunned them both in twenty seconds, and was gone. The locals surmised that he was attending the church revival meeting down the street with his wife and slipped out for a little *Holy Water.*

Another time two stylishly dressed women walked up to the bar and ordered a chilled raspberry martini, extra dry, and a chocolate martini with bitters. Mandy, the bartender, looked at them with a blank stare on her face, shifted her gaze to the dozen beer spigots, and then looked back at the women and said, "Do you know where you are?" They settled for two penny tap beers.

A wide range of people frequent The Tap Inn including construction workers, commercial fishermen, bankers, college students, nurses, lawyers, judges, teachers, retailers, landscapers, farmers, and men and women from all walks of life. Everyone is treated with an equal amount of respect. There were two times, though, when someone walked in and The Tap Inn staff and patrons did a collective gasp.

Singer Jimmy Buffet was raised in Mobile and occasionally visits his hometown. Every few years, Buffet saunters into The Tap Inn and sits in with the house band for a song or two. A guitar autographed by Jimmy Buffet hangs above the back bar.

The other time that someone walked in that brought conversation to a sudden halt was when the front door opened and a curly haired mustachioed man wearing a tweed sport coat with leather patches on the elbows headed straight for the bar – Professor Harlan D. Moscowitz, the Einstein of Kingman University.

"Oh My God!" Mandy the bartender gasped. "Professor Moscowitz is probably going to tell me he changed my Math grade from the "D" he gave me back to the "F" I actually earned."

"Professor Moscowitz, would you care for a drink?" Mandy asked.

"I'd like a chilled raspberry martini, extra dry," Professor Moscowitz said.

"A chilled raspberry martini, extra dry coming right up," Mandy said without hesitation.

Professor Moscowitz took a couple of sips and said, "Very good, Mandy, very good. Just the perfect mathematical proportions of ingredients—very good."

"It's on the house," Mandy said.

"Thank you, but no," Professor Moscowitz said as he dropped a $10 on the bar and said, "keep the change."

I was a mere eight feet from Professor Moscowitz—I was thrilled to see him. I wish I could have yelled out, "Professor Moscowitz, I'm over here in this tin can. That lunkhead Wilfred Fenney spent me on a tap beer, but then, you probably knew that he would."

ooooo

The owner of The Tap Inn, Hank, attributes the bar's

success to one simple concept that he explains this way, "I know what business I'm in. I am not in the business of selling beer and booze. I am in the business of providing people with fun, relaxation, and socialization." To that end, Hank has devised a never-ending array of activities and contests to keep things lively at The Tap Inn.

At least twice a night, at some random time, the bartender rings a bell hanging behind the bar, the patrons let loose with a mournful howl in honor of the moose head above the bar, and the next drink is half price.

One of Hank's best promotions is the first tap beer for a penny. Who drinks just one beer?

Here's another example of Hank's promotions. I'm going to be here at The Tap Inn for at least another three months. How do I know this? Well, because there is a contest to guess how many pennies are in this metal can that I'm in. The winner, to be determined on December 15, gets the metal can and all of us pennies, and bragging rights, as their prize. It costs $1 to enter and so far, there are over 200 entries. Besides knowing how to run a bar, Hank knows how to make money.

ooooo

Watching the people in The Tap Inn is a lot of fun, but even more fun than that is listening to their conversations. Here are a few examples:

Two guys, Frankie and Johnny, are sitting at the bar deep into their third beers. "I quit my job," Frankie says.

"How Come?"

I asked for a raise and they wouldn't give it to me," Frankie replies.

"How much did you ask for?"

"Two dollars a month."

"You asked for a raise of two dollars a month – what in the hell could you do with two extra dollars a month that you can't do now?" Johnny asks.

"Well," Frankie says, "with those two dollars I could have bought myself 300 of these penny beers."

I can almost hear Professor Moscowitz saying, "Lord, take me now."

ooooo

Two guys, Andy and Sam, have been at the bar for about two hours when Andy says, "I went to Sears to try to buy a brand new lawn mower a couple of weeks ago. I didn't have the cash, so they had me fill out a credit application. They called my information in to the Sears Credit Card Department on the spot and they turned me down."

"How come?" Sam asks.

"Well, they never said," Andy replies. "But yesterday, I got a letter from the Sears Credit Card Department and they explained why they turned me down."

"Why was that?" Sam asks.

"They said they turned me down because I am deceased," Andy says.

"How did they find out?" Sam asks. He was dead serious.

ooooo

Two regulars, Leroy and Davie are having a few beers, sitting at the end of the bar, and they get to discussing women.

"Do you still remember your first love?" Davie asks.

"I'll never forget her," Leroy replies as he gazes off into space. "Shelly was her name. It was summertime. I was stuck out on the farm and she was in New Orleans. The highlight of my day was when the mail came because, six days a week, just like clockwork, there was a letter from her.

"Once in a while, though, there would be no letter and my heart would sink. It ruined my whole day. Why didn't she write? Had she found someone new? Was she too busy to write a simple letter? Was she mad? Was it over? But then, the next day, without fail, there would be two letters. Undoubtedly, there had been a mail system glitch that delayed that first letter. But, those were glorious days, with two fresh letters to read and reread and re-reread. It was almost worth the anguish of not having received a letter the day before."

"Was the feeling mutual? Did she love you, too?" Davie asks.

Leroy pauses a moment and then he says, "Naw – she barely knew I existed and if she did know I existed she probably just thought of me as a pest. You see, my older brother, Larry, was nineteen at the time and Shelly was his girlfriend and the letters were written to *him.* I was twelve years old and had just discovered girls, hormones, and sex. Through a little snooping I had also discovered where he hid Shelly's letters in the bottom of a dresser drawer under some newspaper clippings, covered by a pile of socks.

"Since he was nineteen, he was a bonafide farmhand and could drive tractors out in the fields and do all of that stuff. Since I was twelve, and basically worthless when it came to farming, I was relegated to mowing the lawn, chopping weeds, and doing yard work and chores around the house and farm buildings.

"Larry would come home from the field for noon lunch, grab the new letter, and slip upstairs to his room to read it. Then, he came downstairs with a big smile on his face, ate a quick lunch, and headed back out to the fields.

"That was when I struck. As soon as I heard him fire up the tractor, I sneaked upstairs, crept into his room, and peeped out the window to make sure that he hadn't doubled back to the house. Then, being assured that I was all alone with the treasure trove of letters, I slipped my hand under those socks and newspaper clippings and retrieved the day's letter. I became so adept at locating the top letter in the pile without disturbing anything else in the drawer that I could have done it in the dark with my eyes closed.

"Was there some hot stuff in those letters that got your blood boiling?" Davie asks with a smile.

"I still recall it like it was yesterday," Leroy replies. "Remember, I had just discovered girls and sex, and had raging hormones and I lusted for hot, sexy, steamy stuff that would shoot my wad. Day after day, I kept reading, hoping, and praying that one day there would be something in a letter that would fulfill my every fantasy. But it never came. In fact, there usually wasn't even any mushy stuff."

"Did your brother and Shelly end up together?" Davie asks.

"The summer ended and my brother went back to college and he took all of his letters along with him. All of *my* letters with him. And then, for some unexplained reason, he and Shelly broke up a couple of months after that. I suspected that one of them wasn't hot, sexy, and steamy enough for the other, but I never figured out which one."

"It's probably best it ended that way and she didn't marry your brother or you'd have lusted for your sister-in-law the rest of our life," Davie says.

"There's a little more to the story," Leroy says. "About five years later, when I got my own girlfriend who wrote me love letters, I finally figured something out. My girlfriend and I developed our own secret code so we could say hot, sexy, steamy things to each other without anyone else who might read the letters, like my pesky, snoopy younger sister, knowing what we were saying.

"Oh, how I wished I could have again read just one or two of those letters from Shelly to my brother to see if I could crack their secret code. And, I know there was a secret code. Why else would he grab the letter, disappear upstairs to his room for ten or fifteen minutes and come downstairs with a big grin on his face? The lucky dog."

"Now that you and your brother are both grown up, did you ever tell him that you read all of his love letters?" Davie asks.

"Are you nuts?" Leroy says.

ooooo

One afternoon, around five o'clock, the Principal at Jefferson High School, Mr. Samuels, pulls up a bar stool. "I'll have a shot of Jim Beam and the biggest tap beer you've got," he says.

"Rough day?" the bartender asks.

"Let me tell you about it," Mr. Samuels says.

"There's this student, Harold, who's not a bad guy, but he's a little strange. Once in a while, if someone says a word, it's kind of like a secret word that sets him off. For instance, one time, one of his teachers said hoarsely, 'I'm sorry if my voice doesn't carry well today because I have a cold.'

"That set Harold off. 'Cold!' he shouts, 'I'll tell you about being cold. One winter night when I was visiting my Grandmother in Michigan, I got locked out of the house wearing nothing but a pair of shorts and a tee shirt and it was twenty below and I was out there over an hour – that's cold.'

"Another time, a teacher said, 'Working at a second job in addition to a regular job is called *moonlighting*.'

"'Moonlight!' Harold shouted. 'When there's a full moon it can drive some people crazy especially if they're nuts to begin with.'

92

"Once in a while, Harold will fixate on a word and use it three or four times in every sentence, regardless of the topic. There was a time when the word, *particular*, got stuck in his mind. He would say things like 'On this one particular day I got up particularly early and had this particular errand to run so I went to this particular store to get the particular stuff I needed for some particular reason.'

"Usually, after a few days, Harold will wear the word out and stop using it, or another word will get stuck in his mind and replace it, which brings me to today and to the reason I'm in here for a couple of drinks.

"Several teachers, and even a couple of students, reported to me that Harold got a new word stuck in his mind that he was using over and over – *Chickenshit*. It was 'This Chickenshit,' 'That Chickenshit,' 'Them Chickenshits,' 'You Chickenshit,' 'They're Chickenshits,' 'Chickenshit,' 'Chickenshit,' 'Chickenshit.'

"I caught up with Harold and hauled him into my office. Now, even though Harold's antics can be pretty wearing, he is actually pretty harmless and sometimes, as in this case, he most likely didn't know that he was using a bad word.

"I told Harold to have a seat, he sat down, and I closed my office door. Harold hung his head—even he is smart enough to know that if he has been called into the Principal's office, he must have done something bad.

"I started slowly, intent on informing Harold about his bad choice of words and on getting him to stop using the word. I was also cautious not to offend or upset Harold, since he most likely had no idea he was using a bad word and sometimes when he becomes upset, Harold will fall apart.

"'Harold,'" I said, "'I've heard that you have been using a bad word today and it is a bad word that you shouldn't say.'

"Harold hung his head. His eyes looked straight down at the floor. He was embarrassed and seemed afraid that I was about to punish him.

"'You probably don't know that it is a bad word, Harold,'" I said, "'and I'm not mad at you and I'm not going to punish you. But the bad word you've been using is . . . . *Chickenshit*. Did you know that *Chickenshit* is a bad word?' I asked.

"Harold shook his head, slowly, sadly.

"'Do you understand that you shouldn't use that word anymore – that you should not say, Chickenshit?' I asked.

"Harold nodded his head, slowly, sadly.

"'You can go now, Harold,'" I said, "'but just don't use that word anymore.'

"Harold slowly raised his head and looked at me with eyes filled with gratitude. I don't know if it was gratitude for telling him about the bad word or gratitude for not punishing him, but Harold was grateful.

"I rose and Harold likewise rose from his chair and slowly and timidly opened the door, walked out, and closed the door behind himself.

"I thought to myself, 'That went well. I got my message across to Harold, clearly and firmly, and solved the problem without ruffling any feathers.'

"About fifteen seconds later, Harold opened the door to

my office, stuck his head in, looked me squarely in the eye and said, *'Chickenshit.'*

"And, that is why I am here today and why I would like another round."

ooooo

A lot of guys come into The Tap Inn all by themselves, grab a stool near the end of the bar, close to where I am in this tin can, and drown their sorrows. Some of them want to talk about it and they'll tell their story to anyone who will listen. Some don't want to talk at all as they mentally rehash the sorrow that drove them to the bar today. Then there are those who want to talk only to the bartender, apparently believing that after all the sad stories the bartender has heard, they have become somewhat of a barroom psychiatrist.

Take the sad-looking fellow, about fifty years old, who just sat down and ordered a beer.

"How's it going?" the bartender says casually.

"Not so good—I'm feeling pretty low," the guy says.

"Want to talk about it?" the bartender-psychiatrist asks.

The guy is more than willing to talk, after all, that's why he came in here.

"I've been in love with a lot of women in my lifetime," he says. "There was Colette. She was beautiful, petite, and had dazzling dark eyes. She was kind, compassionate, articulate, and fun. We had great conversations on a wide range of topics and she even liked my singing. She once told me so. I loved

95

her. And then it ended. It wasn't my choice."

"I'm sorry to hear that," the bartender-psychiatrist says.

"Then, there was Sheila – she was tall and slender with long, flowing blonde hair. She was smart, kind, fun, and had ambition. She was generous and loved to give gifts. The one gift I'll never forget was that birthday present – a set of bright red satin bedsheets. I know what you are thinking and you are correct. I loved her. It wasn't my choice, but it ended."

"I'm sorry, Pal," the bartender-psychiatrist says.

"Jennifer was stunningly beautiful. She was a star athlete and her body was trim and toned. Any guy who was into sports and/or beautiful women would have adored Jennifer; I was and I did. It wasn't my choice, but it ended."

"Gosh," the bartender-psychiatrist says, "that's too bad."

"Mariska was a very social person and was quite a talker. She could ramble on for 10 or 15 minutes without even taking a breath. She was fun to be around because she told such great stories that always had an outrageous or hilarious ending. Time just flew when you were with Mariska. And then it ended. It wasn't my choice. I loved her."

"Man, I really feel sorry for you," the bartender-psychiatrist says, and he's starting to sound like he really means it.

"Paulette was a professional woman, an accountant. You might think an accountant would be conservative and boring, but not this accountant. Maybe Paulette's most attractive feature was that she loved to party, and I happened to be the kind of guy who loves a party girl. And then it ended. It wasn't my choice."

"I feel your pain," the bartender-psychiatrist says.

"There were others, too – Barbara, Emily, Anna, Caroline, Kathryn, Sally . . . .I loved them all. And, it always ended the same, but it wasn't my choice."

"It's breaking my heart – it really is," the bartender-psychiatrist says. "I don't know how you have survived the beating you've taken."

"Well, here's the deal," the guy says, "all of those women that I loved so madly – Colette, Sheila, Jennifer, Mariska, Paulette, Barbara, Emily, Anna, Caroline, Kathryn, Sally, and the rest of them – they were my *sons'* girlfriends through the years.

"Each of my three sons operate the same way. They date a girl, bring her home to meet mom and dad, and after being around the new girlfriend three or four times, I would fall in love with her. I visualized her marrying my son, of her being the mother of my grandchildren, and of wonderful family outings for years to come.

"And then, just when things seemed to be going so well, my son would dump her. I was devastated. I took it a whole lot harder than my sons seemed to as they went merrily on their way. I love my sons, but they're a bunch of shitheads.

"The reason I'm so downhearted today is that my oldest son actually got engaged a year ago to a magnificent woman, Marilyn. I love her. The wedding was set for three weeks from today and last night my son called it off. What a shithead. Now I have to go through the rest of my life without Marilyn in it."

"You poor bastard," the bartender-psychiatrist says.

"Thanks for listening," the guy says. "I feel better already."

The bartender pours the guy another drink and says, "This one is on the house."

ooooo

Rarely did anyone get kicked out of The Tap Inn, unless they got too rowdy and looked like they might start trouble. There was one exception though. A mild-mannered radio and television shop owner and repairman, Norman, would usually work until around seven and then stop in for three or four drinks before going home. After his second drink, like clockwork, his mind must have flashed back to some of his customers who gave him hell for not getting their radio or television repaired when he said he would. Norman would say, "I'm doing the best I can, that's all I can do." "I'm doing the best I can, that's all I can do." "I'm doing the best I can, that's all I can do," over and over and over again.

After a minute or two of "I'm doing the best I can, that's all I can do," other patrons would move out of earshot of him and soon no one would be sitting at the bar but him. Some people even left to go elsewhere.

Hank, the owner, had warned Norman many times to not say, well, you know, and usually he would knock it off for the rest of the evening.

One night, Norman was at it again and Hank gave him a stern warning to quit saying it or he would have to ask him to leave. Norman replied, "Ok, Ok, I'm doing the best I can, that's all I can do."

That's when Hank gave mild-mannered Norman the Heave-Ho and banned him from entering The Tap Inn ever again.

Thank you, Hank, but I wish you had done it sooner. But, I know you're doing the best you can, and that's all you can do.

ooooo

The weeks have flown by and I am starting to dread December 15, when the winner of the contest to guess how many pennies are in this metal can will be determined and the winner will get the can and all of its contents, including me. Then, who knows what will happen. Will I end up in a penny hoarder's collection? Will the winner of the contest be a hunter who melts all of us pennies down to make slugs for deer season? Will I sit in a coffee can in the corner of someone's garage for decades? Will I end up in the hands of another person who is famous, like Mookey and Blaize Cameron? Will I end up in a box of junk that gets hauled to the dump grounds? I've been through this situation before, and it's a scary time.

ooooo

Tonight's the night. One of the bar's regular customers, a banker, brought in an automatic coin counter and the contents of the metal can, including me, will be dumped into it to be counted.

There are more than 1,200 entries, at $1 each, with guesses ranging from 267 to 125,001 pennies.

There are over 300 people in The Tap Inn for the big event. To commemorate the event, tap beers are a penny every time the bartender rings the bell behind the bar.

We are dumped into the coin counter and it whirs and clanks for about five minutes until all of us pennies have been run through it. The actual count is 4,816 pennies in the metal can. The nearest guess was 4,900 by one of the regulars, Andy, the guy who was turned down for credit when he wanted to buy a lawn mower because the credit card company determined that he is deceased. That small technicality did not stop Andy from developing the perfect strategy for winning the contest. Every other day for the past 100 days, Andy entered a new guess, at $1 per entry.

Andy is ecstatic. Hopefully, it will never occur to him to calculate the monetary amount of his winnings, which was a net loss of $1.84, after deducting his winnings valued at $48.16 from the cost of his entries, $50. But, the contest is not about money—it's about bragging rights and Andy will have those rights until next December 15 when the new contest is held.

All of us pennies have been dumped back into the metal can and Andy grabs the can with both hands. He walks around the bar and doles out one penny to every person in the place. Even Andy was able to figure out it would be cheaper to give everyone a penny than to buy the house a round at regular prices.

Andy hands me to a nice-looking woman about twenty-five years old who is with a handsome man about her same age. I cannot help but notice the way she is dressed – she has on a long-sleeved white blouse with a magnificent crest stitched into the pocket with gold thread. Her denim jeans have similar gold stitching down the outside of the pants legs and she is wearing a lightweight pale yellow jacket with a crest on its shoulder that matches the crest on her blouse pocket. There are around three hundred people in here tonight and she is the class of the place.

The woman takes me from Andy, slowly examines my shiny beauty, both front and back, and slips me into the small purse hanging from a strap on her shoulder.

If I could have picked one person in this place to start my new adventure with, it would have been her. I am one lucky penny.

Golden Threads and Silver Needles

It is 6:00 a.m. and I am still in the purse of the woman who received me from Andy at The Tap Inn last night. The purse is on a shelf in a closet in what used to be a small bedroom that is now apparently a small sewing room. Five shelves have been installed in the closet. Bolts of cloth are stacked on three shelves and spools of various colors of thread are lined up on another shelf.

She is drawing something on a sheet of paper when she hears footsteps coming down the hallway. She grabs the piece of paper and quickly slips it into an open drawer of her sewing table and closes the drawer just as her husband appears in the doorway.

"What are you doing? He asks with a tinge of accusation in his voice.

"Nothing," she replies with a tinge of defiance in her voice.

"Got a lot of work to do today?" he asks.

"I've got three alterations to do for Casey Peterson and I've got to get started on the five bridesmaid's dresses for Jaci Rose. I'll be busy into the night," she replies.

He walks over to where she is seated behind the Singer sewing machine and gives her a hug and a kiss. "Have a good day, Haley; I'll see you around six. Love you."

"Love you, too, Rick," she says.

Rick starts singing as he walks down the hallway and Haley can hear him even after he leaves the house and gets into his truck, "A-shrimpin' I will go, a-shrimpin' I will go, even if the tide is low, a-shrimpin' I will go."

Haley smiles, turns off her sewing machine, grabs the piece of paper from the sewing table drawer, and continues with the sketch she was working on before Rick interrupted her.

At precisely eight o'clock, Haley puts her sketch back in the drawer, turns on the sewing machine, grabs a blouse and a scissors and goes to work. Within fifteen minutes she has turned a beautiful long-sleeved blouse into a beautiful short-sleeved blouse. In another half hour she has the other two alterations finished.

Haley grabs a bolt of blue satin material from the closet. Within three hours, it is transformed into a beautiful bridesmaid dress that would rival any dress in the fanciest bridal shops in Beverly Hills.

At a few minutes after two in the afternoon, Haley's sister, Jill, stops by the house with an envelope for Haley.

The sisters chat about the weather and last night's party at The Tap Inn. Haley tells her sister that she received a beautiful, shiny penny from the winner of the contest.

Hey, it wouldn't hurt to show me off a little bit.

Jill hands the envelope to Haley; it is from Manley Fashion Designs in Los Angeles. Haley rips open the envelope and removes the letter. She starts reading out loud, "Dear Haley, Although your work has considerable merit, we are sorry to inform you that . . . ."

Haley stops reading, "Another rejection," she says.

"That's rejection number thirty-seven. I guess my ideas just aren't flashy enough or upscale enough for the houses in New York City, Los Angeles, and San Francisco."

"Your ideas are great," Jill says. "Maybe you're ahead of your time, but keep at it and one day the world will catch up to you."

"I don't know," a dejected Haley says. "Maybe Rick is right—I should give up this nonsense and stick to my sewing and alterations."

"But, it's your passion, it's your dream," Jill says.

"It is my dream, but not everybody gets to live their dreams," Haley says.

"Has Rick been hounding you about it again?" Jill asks.

"He's always trying to catch me working on it—he thinks I'm wasting my time," Haley said.

"Look, you work on your sewing eight or nine hours a day six days a week. You're entitled to some free time to do what you want."

"That might be true," Haley says, "but on the other hand, it's not right for me to sneak around behind my husband's back, working on it when he's not around. And, it's not right using your return address so he doesn't find out I'm still sending out proposals."

"If he can't support you and won't encourage you to

chase our dreams, at least he could stay neutral and keep out of your way," Jill says.

"It isn't that Rick doesn't have dreams, because he does. He has dreams for both of us, big dreams," Haley says. "If he works on the shrimp boat for ten years and I work hard on my sewing and alterations, we can buy our own shrimp boat. We'll be able to buy our own house and Rick's got it figured out that if there isn't any disaster in the Gulf, like another oil spill, we can buy another shrimp boat in three or four years and then another and another until we have a whole fleet of them. He has big dreams, and I'm part of it. It's our dreams."

"Rick's a great guy and I love him," Jill says. "I just wish he had a little more faith in you," Jill says.

"We'll be okay," Haley says.

ooooo

Rick arrives home at 6:10 and Haley stashes her sheets of paper in the drawer when she hears his truck pull up.

Rick walks in, goes straight to Haley's sewing room and gives her a big hug and a kiss. "Busy day?" He asks.

"Got three alterations and two bridesmaid's dresses done. I should finish the other dresses tomorrow."

"You deserve a break," he says with a smile. "Let's go to the Pink Pony for a burger and a beer. Bill Carpenter's playing tonight from six to nine."

"I'm in," Haley says, and they are off.

ooooo

It is 6:00 a.m. and Haley is at her favorite place in the whole world - her sewing table in her nice, cozy sewing room. She is concentrating on a sketch and doesn't hear Rick coming down the hallway in his stockings.

"What are you doing?" Rick says with an accusing tone.

"I'm just designing a dress for EllenGray Fitzgibbons for the New Year Eve's ball at the Palladium in Mobile," Haley lies. "Here," she says holding it up, "take a look. Do you think she'll like it?"

"Looks good to me," Rick says. He gives Haley a quick hug and a kiss and is on his way, singing, "A-shrimpin' I will go, a-shrimpin' I will go, even if the tide is low, a-shrimpin' I will go."

Haley takes a deep breath and slowly blows the air out of her mouth, "That was close," she says to herself. And then, she goes back to work on the sketch.

ooooo

At shortly after two in the afternoon, Haley's sister, knocks on the front door and charges in without waiting for Haley to open it. She holds a letter in her hand. "This came special delivery," she says. "I have a good feeling about this one."

"Special delivery, that's as high-classed a rejection as you can get!" Haley says with a smile.

Haley looks at the return address and says, "Oh, my God – Atteberry Fashions – Oh, my God!"

Haley rips open the envelope and begins reading aloud, "Dear Haley, We love your fashion designs. They are fresh, new, and wonderful. Please call me at your earliest convenience at 212-327-4466. Sincerely, William Atteberry, President, Atteberry Fashions.

Jill is screaming but Haley is just sitting in her chair motionless, stunned.

"Give him a call, give him a call," Jill shouts. "I can't stand the suspense."

"Atteberry Fashions is the most prestigious designer of women's clothing in the United States and is one of the top three fashion houses in the whole world," Haley says. "This must be a joke – or a mistake. They couldn't be interested in me – in my designs – it's gotta be a mistake."

"Give him a call and find out," Jill says.

Jill's not the only one who can't stand the suspense. I'm over here in her purse on the shelf and I'm going crazy—well, as crazy as a penny can get.

Haley picks up the phone, takes a deep breath, and dials. A moment later, Haley's face lights up and she begins talking, "Hello, I received a letter saying I should dial this number for Mr. William Atteberry; my name is Haley and I'm from Gulf Shores, Alabama and . . ."

Haley is interrupted by a voice on the other end of the line, "Yes, sir, Mr. Atteberry" ... "Thank you very much, Mr.

Atteberry"... "Bill..." "You want me to call you Bill?"... "Thank you"... "Yes, I have many more designs"... "Yes, over a hundred"... "Yes, I'd love to sign an exclusive contract with Atteberry Fashions"... "Yes, I do have some questions. First of all, My husband and I live in Gulf Shores, Alabama - we don't want to move to New York City, in fact, we *won't* move to New York City" ... "Really?"... "Really?" ... "That would be perfect, absolutely perfect"... "Yes, I could do that—can my husband come along?" ... "You do?" ... "That would be perfect. When?" ... "After the holidays, February?" ... "Please say that again"... "How many?"... "Would you say that again"... "Okay, Mr. Atteberry, I'll"... "I'm sorry, Bill, I'll call you tomorrow after I have had a chance to discuss this with my husband tonight"... "I'm sure he will, he's a wonderful man"... "Thank you, Bill, so very much" ... "It was nice talking to you, too... Goodbye."

Haley hangs up the phone and bursts into tears and cries like a baby for a full minute. Jill walks over to her and hugs her tightly.

"Jill, it's everything that I dreamed about. Everything," Haley says. "He doesn't want me to move to New York City— in fact, he said he wouldn't allow it even if I wanted to. Mr. Atteberry, Bill, said he is afraid my living there, seeing the same things the New York fashion designers see every day, talking to the people they talk to every day, eating the same places they eat every day, riding the same subways and cabs they ride every day – well, I'd soon become one of them and would lose my inspiration that comes from my roots right here in Gulf Shores."

"Money," Jill says, "did he say anything about money?"

"I made him repeat it twice," Haley says. "He said he'll pay me $50,000 for signing the contract and then I'll earn two percent of their gross sales of my designs, world wide."

"How many do they sell a year?" Jill asked.

"I made him repeat it twice, and I still can't believe it," Haley says. "He said they might sell several thousand pieces a year."

"And you get two percent of their gross sales – that could be tens of thousands of dollars a year!" Jill says with a huge smile on her face.

"That's what he said," Haley says. "I can't believe it."

"Good for you," Jill says. "You earned it and you deserve it. I'm very, very proud of you and very happy for you."

"Well, Jill," Haley says, "you're going to be right there with me. You taught me how to sew and how to turn an idea into a concept that became a design. You're in it with me."

"What about Rick?" Jill says. "What if he fights you on this?"

"I hope it doesn't come to that, where I'll have to choose between the two great loves of my life – my dream of designing fashions and my dream of spending my life with Rick," Haley says.

Haley thinks for a moment and then she says, "I guess it will come down to this – if Rick loves me enough to support me and encourage me to pursue my passion for fashion."

ooooo

It is about 6:15 p.m. and Haley can hear Rick's truck pull up outside the house. Haley continues working on a drawing on her sewing table.

Rick walks in and says, "Hello, love of my life. . . ."

He stops in mid sentence when he sees that Haley is drawing a design for a women's blouse. "What are you doing?" he asks.

Haley holds the sheet of paper up for Rick to see. "I'm creating a design that I plan to send off to a fashion house in New York City."

"Oh, Baby, why waste your time on all of that – you know they've got thousands of designers in New York City and San Francisco and those other places you send your designs off to – you're just wasting your time and they're just going to turn you down and beat you down and break your heart. Give it up."

"Rick," Haley says firmly, "what is the real reason you don't want me to create my designs and to try to catch on with some fashion house as a designer? What is it?"

"Like I said," Rick says, "it's a tough row to hoe and they'll just turn you down and reject your work and break your heart."

"Ricky," Haley says firmly with fire in her eyes, "there is more to it than that and I want to know what it is – why don't you support me and encourage me – why do you want me to fail?"

"Baby," Rick pleads, "I don't want you to fail – I want you to do good. I want you to be happy in what you do but…" Rick's voice trails off.

"But what?" Haley says softly. "Tell me – but what? Tell me."

Rick looks down at the floor with a mournful look on his face, "I'm just a shrimper, that's all. Maybe that's all I'll ever be. But the one thing really, really special I've got going for me is you, Haley, it's you. It's the one thing in my life that really means anything to me. Your designs are great, they're special. I know they are because when you wear the clothes you design and sew, women just go crazy over them. They're better than anything else out there.

"If you keep sending your designs off to those fashion places, sooner or later one of them is going to see your talent and offer you a job and then you'll move off to New York City or San Francisco – and I can't live in one of those places – I'm a country boy. And, we'll be done. You'll be in one of those cities working with all those fancy designers and I'll be here and we'll be done. And, I don't want us to be done."

"That's it?" Haley says, with a mystified look on her face. "That's it? That's why you don't want me to draw my designs – that you think I'll go off and leave you behind? Or want to drag you along?"

"That's about it," Rick says.

"What if I could hook up with one of those big fashion houses in one of those cities but could work from right here in Gulf Shores and would never even have to go there?" Haley asked.

"Work from here and not move there? Shoot, that would be great! If you could do that, I'd say go for it, and I'd be right there behind you, pushing you and helping you," Rick said.

"Rick," Haley says with a smile on her face, "you're an idiot, but you're the idiot that I love. Come over here—I've got something to tell you."

I know that I'm not supposed to cry, but if I could I would right now. And, Haley is right, Rick – you are an idiot.

ooooo

Haley and Rick gawk around like two country bumkins in the big city, which they are. It is the middle of February and they have been in New York City for three days and are taking a walk on the bustling sidewalk along 37th Street before they are to meet Bill Atteberry back at the St. Moritz Hotel on Central Park, where they have been staying. True to her roots, Haley is wearing an outfit that she designed and sewed herself, which has been drawing stares and compliments from the high-end crowd in Manhattan. Also true to her roots, Haley has the same purse slung over her shoulder that she has used for the past two years, which is why I am here in New York City, also.

Bill Atteberry, one of the busiest and most successful icons in the fashion world, has been Haley and Rick's personal tour guide for most of their three days in the city. He took them to the Statue of Liberty, World Trade Center,

New York Stock Exchange, and Times Square. They saw a Broadway play, Death of A Salesman, and dined at Tavern on the Green and ate New York style pizza.

They spent an entire afternoon in the Garment District in Manhattan, where Bill Atteberry gave them a tour of his extensive office complex, design area, and garment manufacturing facilities.

At the end of the second day, Atteberry proudly asked, "Well, Rick, what do you think of New York City?"

"I like it, I really do," Rick said. "I don't think I'd want to live here, but I wouldn't mind coming back for a visit once in a while."

"And you, Haley?" Atteberry asked.

"I feel exactly the same way, Bill," she said. "We are having a grand time and hope we can come back again sometime, but we live in Gulf Shores, Alabama – that's where we belong."

"And, that's where I want you to be," Atteberry said.

Haley and Rick continue their walk and come across a man sitting along the sidewalk on a folding chair, strumming his guitar, singing Bob Dylan's "Blowin' in the Wind." His clothes are unkempt, his shoes have a hole in the top, and probably the bottom, and he wears dark sunglasses. His open guitar case has a hand-written sign proclaiming, "Blind and singing for your pleasure." A few quarters, dimes, nickels, and pennies, rest in the bottom of his case. Kind-hearted Haley unzips her purse and reaches in the bottom and grabs a handful of coins, including me. She walks over to the blind man's guitar case and . . . .

"No, No, No," I would like to scream out, "Don't leave me here with this guy, please." But, of course, I'm only a penny and— Oh, oh, I feel myself falling.

ooooo

That is the last time that I saw Haley and Rick. They were great. I do not know what happened to Haley's fashion design career, but, ladies, if you check the labels in your closet, I have a strong feeling that more than one of them will say, "A Haley Grummond Design."

Miracle on Thirty-Seventh Street

I have been in this guitar case for nearly two hours and after every song, and sometimes during songs, people drop their change into the case. Sometimes a dollar bill or even a five is thrown in.

The singer's name is Willie T. I know this because after every two or three songs he does a little self-promoting to coax money out of the bystanders.

"You're listening to Willie T, the finest folk singer on 37th street, and possibly the finest folk singer in all of New York City. As you can see from my sign over there. . . ." Willie T pauses and points in the general direction of the sign in his guitar case, "I can't see you, but I can hear you if you clap for me and if you drop some change in the guitar case. In fact, my ears are so finely tuned that I can hear it if you drop a ten or twenty into the case, and I can tell which is which."

That usually brings out a few chuckles and a few bucks as Willie T launches into the next song. Willie T's a good guitar player and a darn good singer, and is streetwise enough to limit his songs to no more three minutes each to increase the number of times he can coax some money from the audience.

Willie T's repertoire includes "Mr. Bojangles," "If I Had A Hammer," "John Henry," "Where Have All the Flowers

Gone," "Stewball," "Sweet Betsy From Pike," "500 Miles," and "Lemon Tree," among many classics from the folk music scene of the 60's and 70's.

I'm really getting into the swing of Willie T's show and enjoying it a lot when he announces, "Well, folks, it's time for Willie T to take a little pause for the cause. I'll be back in just a little while," and with that he closes out with a foot-stompin' version of "The Midnight Special."

Willie T rests his guitar against the edge of the case and scoops up the coins, including me, and the bills, and puts us in the pocket of his jacket and zips it up. He puts his guitar in its case, folds up his little chair, grabs his white cane, and slowly joins the throng of people hustling along the sidewalk.

When Willie T gets about a half block from where he was performing, he stops, turns his head from side to side, pulls off his dark sunglasses, folds up his telescoping white cane, and takes off at a pace that could qualify him for the hundred yard dash in the Olympics.

Halleluja! It's a miracle! Willie T has been healed! He can see! The blind man can see!

Willie T ducks into Bernardo's Bagles, stashes his guitar, chair, and cane by a table along the side and goes to the counter to order.

"Willie T, my man" the guy behind the counter says. "How's it going today – makin' lots of money?"

"Ah, not too bad, Bernardo," Willie T says as he slaps his jacket pocket containing me and the other loot.

"I keep telling you, Willie T, get a dog, you'll increase

your take by fifty percent. My wife's second cousin, Alfanso, has a dog and he's rakin' in the dough. He's an odd duck and on his own nobody would give him a dime, but people feel sorry for his dog and just throw money at him. Get a dog—people will think it's a seeing-eye dog and you'll get a lot of sympathy."

"I'd rather they tip me because they like my music rather than they tip me because of sympathy," Willie T says.

"And the blind man gimmick—that's not for sympathy?" Bernardo says.

"Hey, everybody expects a folk singer to be blind, it's part of the image," Willie T says.

"Willie T, it's blues singers who is blind; folk singers wear goofy hats. Get a dog."

"One gimmick at a time," Willie T responds. "Now, shut up and give me a blueberry bagel with cream cheese and a cup of black coffee, and don't skimp on the cream cheese like you did yesterday."

"Always complaining, you musicians and you blind guys, always complaining," Bernardo says. "That'll be three dollars and forty-six cents."

"What the hell, the price go up since yesterday?" Willie T says.

"It's been the same price for ten years. Just pay it and go sit down—you're turning my high-class place into a slum," Bernardo says.

Willie T unzips his jacket pocket and pulls out two dollar bills and a handful of change, which he lays on the counter.

He slowly sorts out the exact change, which includes me.

My life with Willie T lasted for a little over two hours.

It was a good gig, Willie T. I wish I could hear you sing "Sweet Betsy From Pike," just one more time. Your act may not need a dog, but a goofy hat. . . ., well, maybe.

Taking a Bite
Out of the Big Apple

For the past three months I have been on the move constantly, changing hands as many as twenty times in a single day here in The Big Apple. I have passed through the hands of cab drivers, Broadway performers, a professional basketball player, drunks, preachers, pimps, teachers, shopkeepers, accountants, politicians, truck drivers, longshoremen, fashion models, police officers, custodians, drug dealers, nurses, chefs, waitresses, musicians, firemen, construction workers, hot dog vendors, carnival operators, hookers, mechanics, authors, bartenders, a professional baseball player, stockbrokers, lawyers, literary agents, and numerous tourists from all over the world.

I've been to Manhattan, Queens, Brooklyn, Staten Island, The Bronx, Greenwich Village, Little Italy, Chinatown, and even New Jersey. And culture, let me tell you about culture: I've been to Carnegie Hall, Broadway plays, the Metropolitan Museum of Art, and St. Patrick's Cathedral.

I went on shopping trips to Macy's, Tiffany's, Sak's Fifth Avenue, and Hiram's Used Hats, Shoes, Belts, and Handbags.

I went to a New York Knicks game, saw the Mets and Yankees play, visited The Bronx Zoo, rode the Staten Island

Ferry, and rode The Cyclone at Coney Island.

I've ridden in limousines, taxis, street sweepers, horse-drawn carriages, bulldozers, subways, buses, trains, boats, and a rickshaw.

I've been to dozens of high-class night clubs and discos where you had to know the doorman or give him a big tip to get in and I've been to dives so dark you couldn't see the drunks passed out on the floor.

I've been with people who slept in penthouses and with people who slept in the gutter.

I have seen more of the Big Apple than most of the people who were born and raised here, I'd guess, and I've had a ball. Well, for the most part, except for a couple of times I was dropped on the sidewalk and stepped on by hundreds of shoes before some good soul picked me up and polished me up.

Then, there was the time that nitwit bet his buddy I'd dissolve in three minutes if he dropped me into his Windsor-Coke. I'm glad the asshole lost his bet and it was pretty funny when he damn near choked on me when he forgot I was still in his glass.

ooooo

This morning, I started out in the pants pocket of a pair of jeans worn by a man who is in The City for the "Pumpers'" convention. As he happily explained to the sweet young waitress at Demarco's Sidewalk Cafe, "Pumper" is short for

"Shit Pumper," which is slang for guys who pump septic tanks and rent out port-a-pots. "The business stinks," he says as he laughs his fool head off – Pumper humor.

For the past eight years, the Pumpers' convention had been held in Oklahoma City, but the board of the National Pumper's Association decided it was time to elevate the image of the Pumpers, so they moved it to New York City as an experiment. From the grin on Pumper Guy's face, it looks like he might have been elevated.

"Isn't that kind of a crappy job?" the waitress says with a smile.

"It is," Pumper Guy says, and then he motions for her to come closer so he can whisper in her ear. "But, you can make a shitload of money."

To prove his point, Pumper Guy leaves her a $100 bill and all the change in his pocket, including me, in payment of his $26 check. That, indeed, will elevate one's image.

After Pumper Guy leaves, the waitress scoops up the $100 and all the change, which is almost too much for her small hand. As she turns to walk away, I fall from her grasp and land on the seat of Pumper Guy's chair. She doesn't notice that I am gone.

ooooo

Two women in their mid thirties, wearing brightly colored dresses and stylish hats with broad brims, enter the sidewalk cafe and are seated at the table that Pumper Guy has just vacated.

"Well, look at my good fortune," one of them says with a smooth southern drawl, "I just found a lucky penny. It's bright and shiny and I'm going to put it in my purse and take it back home with me."

"Good morning, ladies," the waitress says. "I just love your hats. Where are you ladies from?"

"I'm Savanah and this is Mary Kate, and we're from Chaleston, South Carolina," she says.

"Charleston?" the waitress asks.

"Honey," Savannah says with that slow southern drawl, "there may be an "R" in Charleston when they write it, but when you say it, there is no "R" in Chaleston." She and Mary Kate laugh and the waitress joins in.

"Are you in The City for long?" the waitress asks.

"We've been here three days and have shopped and shopped until our husbands are going to have to go out and get a second job to pay for it all," Mary Kate says. "Our plane leaves at three this afternoon, but we had such a wonderful time and we will be back."

Savannah and Mary Kate finish their breakfast and the waitress brings them the check.

"It was a pleasure meeting you ladies," she says, "and have a wonderful trip back to – to Chaleston."

ooooo

At 3:05, Savannah and Mary Kate board the plane and

are on their way, back to *Chaleston.*

New York City . . . .thanks for the sights, the sounds, the energy, the hustle, the bustle, the people, the culture, the fun, and the memories. I've seen so much, yet I've seen so little.

I am glad that I'm a penny and do not need to eat, drink, rest, or sleep, or I would have been dead by now from the pace that you put me through over the past three months. I don't know how or when, but I'll be back.

The Revs

It is 5:05 in the afternoon when Savannah and Mary Kate's plane arrives at Charleston International Airport. By 6:00 they are in Mary Kate's car and headed for home. Along the way, they stop at a Quick Sack convenience store for some snacks. Savannah's total comes to $2.43 and she digs in her coin compartment for change. She fishes out a quarter, dime, nickel, and three pennies, including me and within seconds I am in the cash register drawer.

Savannah and Mary Kate, it was a pleasure meeting you Southern Belles, and thanks for letting me hitch a ride with you to Chaleston.

ooooo

A southern gentleman holds the door for Savannah and Mary Kate as they leave the Quick Sack. He grabs a six pack of Bud Light and a bag of pretzels and gives the clerk ten dollars. The total is $7.49 and he receives two dollars, two quarters and one penny in change. I am the penny. He stashes the two dollar bills in his wallet and puts the two quarters and me in the coin compartment.

The guy, who's maybe around 30 years old, hops in his pickup truck and away we go. A half hour, three Bud Lights, and a bag of pretzels later, we are entering the city limits of Goose Creek, South Carolina.

We pull up in front of a double garage that someone has remodeled into a replica of a vintage gas station, complete with three old-time gas pumps out in front of the building.

He hops out of the pickup, grabs the three remaining Bud Lights, and joins the two guys who are sitting at a table made from a sheet of plywood resting on two old cracker barrels.

"It's about time you get here, Bubba," one of the guys says.

You're kidding me, right? The first guy I meet in the state of South Carolina is named "Bubba." How cool is that!

"Jim Bob, Billy Ray," Bubba says, "how's it goin'."

You're putting me on, right? The second guy I meet in the state of South Carolina is named "Jim Bob" and the third guy I meet in the state of South Carolina is named "Billy Ray." Doubly cool!

"Have a good time hangin' out with your brother in Chaleston?" Billy Ray asks.

"Ya, a real good time. We went out and shot some pool and drank some beer with a couple of his buddies he met on the job. They were pretty interesting guys," Bubba says.

"How's that?" Jim Bob asks.

"Well, in addition to their regular jobs building houses, they've all got side jobs to make some extra money," Bubba says. "They're buying new hunting rifles and fishing gear and all sorts of stuff with money from their side jobs."

"What kind of side jobs?" Billy Ray asks.

"Crazy stuff most people would never think of. The one guy went to a one-week hypnosis program and learned how to hypnotize people," Bubba says.

"No shit!" Billy Ray says.

"On Saturday nights he performs in night clubs in Chaleston. He gets people up on stage and hypnotizes them and gets them to squawk like chickens, and flop around on the floor like a bunch of beached whales. Then, he makes them think their shoes are on fire or they're in the desert and are dying of thirst.

"I went to see him with my brother. The guy's pretty good. Oh, and then his girlfriend, who's real pretty, wears a long dress and goes around the audience and nudges people, to make it look like he's put the whole damn place out and she's got to wake 'em up. Funny as hell!" Bubba says.

"How much does he get paid?" Jim Bob asks.

"He gets $200 a night for two 45-minute shows."

"Are you kidding me?" Billy Ray says.

"Cash, they paid him in cash, and I was there and saw the manager count out two $100 bills," Bubba says.

"How about the other guys, what are they doing for side jobs?" Jim Bob asks.

"Even though this guy, Ted, is swingin' a nine pound hammer and bending nails, he's a mathematical genius. My brother said he's slightly autistic – you know those guys can make numbers dance. Anyway, he's got this deal he does with a penny and he's making $50 to $100 a night and he can do it anywhere – in a restaurant, bar, bus depot, airport – anywhere he can strike up a conversation with someone," Bubba says.

"With a penny? What's he do?" Billy Ray asks.

"Well, he's got two deals. Here's the first one. You might think that if you flipped a penny 1,000 times it would even out and come up heads 500 times and come up tails 500 times, right?" Bubba says.

"Ya, the *Law of Averages*. I learned that in grade school," Billy Ray says.

"Well, this genius, Ted, figured out that isn't true. Whatever side of the coin is facing up before you flip it will come up just a little bit more often than the side that is facing down. So, Ted strikes up a conversation with somebody and eventually asks the guy if he'd like to place a friendly wager of, say $10, on which will come up the most often out of twenty flips of a penny – heads or tails. He even suggests they use the other guy's penny so the guy doesn't think Ted's got a trick penny. Well, Ted normally wins and then gives the guy a chance to break even – double or nothing. Before the guy knows it, he's lost $30 or $40 to Ted."

"Wow! That's like picking money up off the ground," Jim Bob says.

"That's nothin'," Bubba says. "Where he really makes his money, is his other trick with a penny. Now, on a penny, Lincoln's head is one side and the Lincoln Memorial is on the other side. Ted bets a guy, say $10 or $20, that if he spins a penny, say twenty times, the Lincoln Memorial will come up more often than Lincoln's head.

"Now, here's the secret that Ted figured out," Bubba says, "the side of the penny with Lincoln's head is slightly heavier than the side with the Lincoln Memorial, so when the penny stops spinning, three out of four times the penny will land face side down, with the Lincoln Memorial side up."

You're kidding me! I'm lopsided? Tell me more, Bubba.

"You're right, that Ted is a bloomin' genius," Billy Ray says.

"And then, there's the third guy, Roger. Somehow he found out that he could become a *Marriage Minister* by sending off $9.95 to some company and they sent him a certificate. With that certificate, he says he's legal to perform marriages, and he does, at $100 a pop. He performs about twenty-five weddings a year," Bubba says.

"For $9.95 he became a minister—a pastor?" Jim Bob says.

"Could we do that, too, just for the fun of it?" Billy Ray says.

"I suspect we could," Bubba says.

The three of them look at each other like three light bulbs have just been turned on, and the decision is made— they will become *Men of the Cloth*, sort of.

ooooo

Within ten days of sending off their checks, Bubba receives the three *Marriage Minister Certificates* in the mail. They are impressive, suitable for framing. Included are

131

instructions on how to conduct a proper wedding and there is even sample wording that they can use - "Dearly Beloved. . . ." and things like that.

Every time the three guys get together, they take delight in calling themselves and each other by their professional Marriage Minister names, Brother Bubba, Reverend Billy Ray, and Pastor Jim Bob. They break out the Holy Water, that tastes a lot like beer, and have a regular revival meeting.

Well, it wasn't long before the three Reverends decided they should have areas of ministerial specialization. Brother Bubba would handle confessions, Reverend Billy Ray would offer forgiveness, and Pastor Jim Bob would administer circumcisions with a retooled apple peeler.

One night, inspired by an eighteen pack of Holy Water, the three Reverends come up with a money-making program that will put the side jobs of those house builders in Charleston to shame.

The three Marriage Ministers would offer the "Ten-Day Revocable Marriage." Here's how it would work: they would charge a couple $100 to get married. After the honeymoon, if they still wanted to be married, the Marriage Ministers would take the marriage certificate to the courthouse and file it for them, making it official.

On the other hand, if after the honeymoon, the couple discovered that the idea of being saddled with each other forever made them violently ill, for an additional fee of $500, the Marriage Ministers would shred the marriage certificate and the couple could each go their own way as if nothing had happened. Faster and cheaper than a divorce, you've got to admit.

Of course, Brother Bubba, Reverend Billy Ray, and Pastor Jim Bob had no intention of ever doing anything. It was all a private joke among the three of them. They would conduct no weddings, hear no confessions, offer no forgiveness, and perform no circumcisions. They were just talking big and having a little fun.

That is, until one evening in a nightclub an acquaintance, Holly, says to Bubba, "I understand that Billy Ray, Jim Bob, and you are Marriage Ministers."

"Yes, we are," Bubba replies proudly with a smile on his face.

"Well," Holly says, "I just got engaged to this guy, Dale, and we'd like you to marry us."

"Ha, ha, ha," Bubba replies, "that's funny, ha, ha."

"I'm serious," Holly says. And, either she was or she is a damn good actor.

"You can't be serious," Bubba replies.

"Well, I am," Holly says firmly.

"It wouldn't be legal," Bubba says, trying to squirm out of it. "I paid $9.95 for a mail order Marriage Minister Certificate. It can't be legal."

"It is. I've been to lots of weddings conducted by Marriage Ministers like you."

"How about Billy Ray or Jim Bob, they're Marriage Ministers, too," Bubba says.

"Billy Ray would talk too much and Jim Bob might not

show up; I want you to marry us."

Holly was resolute that Bubba should be the one to marry her and Dale, probably because she figured he'd keep it short and do it for free.

Finally, Holly wore Bubba down and he conceded that he would go to the courthouse to see if his $9.95 mail order Marriage Minister Certificate allowed him to perform binding marriages. He assured Holly that if it did, he would marry them. He was that certain it would not be legal and he'd be off the hook.

∞∞∞

Bubba sheepishly approaches a clerk at the Recorder's counter in the courthouse, pulls out his mail order Marriage Minister Certificate, hands it to the clerk and says, "Please don't laugh at me, but I bought this *Marriage Minister Certificate* by mail order for $9.95 and now someone has asked me to marry them. It's not legal and binding, right?"

The clerk studies the Marriage Minister Certificate and says, "Yes it is."

"W-h-a-a-t?" Bubba exclaims in disbelief.

"It's legal and binding. The couple getting married comes in here and picks up the marriage certificate prior to the wedding, after you conduct the wedding, you sign the certificate, and they bring it in here and file it. That's all there is to it."

"You're putting me on, right?" Bubba says.

"In fact, we have a list of about a dozen Marriage Ministers like you and people who are planning on getting married often stop in and pick someone from the list to do the job. Do you want me to add your name to the list?"

"N-o-o-o!" Bubba groans.

"Well, then, you're all set, *Reverend,*" the clerk says with a little smile on her face.

"Smartass," Bubba mutters to himself as he leaves the Recorder's office.

So, it was decided—Brother Bubba was going to marry Holly and Dale, but he has a problem.

ooooo

The problem, as Bubba explains it to Jim Bob and Billy Ray is this: "I knew Holly and her first husband, Henry, pretty well. Hell, I even went to their wedding and danced with Holly at their wedding dance. I used to run into Holly and Henry all the time before it all fell apart. Holly and Henry—it had a nice flow to it and the names sounded like they belonged together. For five years it was Holly and Henry, Holly and Henry, Holly and Henry. Now, this new guy, Dale, comes along. I've never even met him, but 'Holly and Dale' – it just doesn't sound right, it doesn't have a good rhythm to it.

"I'm afraid I'm going to screw it up and say something like, 'I now pronounce Holly and Henry husband and wife,' and leave that poor bastard, Dale, just standing there wondering how he fits into all this."

"Aw, you'll do okay," Billy Ray says. "You're worrying over nothing."

"They're getting married in ten days, and I've been practicing," Bubba says. "All day long I repeat to myself 'Holly and Dale, Holly and Dale, Holly and Dale, Holly and Henry. . . .dammit, I did it again.

"When I go to bed at night, I say to myself, 'Don't say Henry, don't say Henry, don't say Henry, don't say Henry.' And, the more I say 'Don't say Henry,' the more I'm afraid I'm going to say it – the more I'm sure I'm going to say it, in front of Holly and all of her relatives and friends and in front of that poor bastard, Dale. He deserves better."

ooooo

Finally, the day of the blessed event arrives. Bubba is sweating bullets and keeps rehearsing, "Holly and Dale, Holly and Dale, Holly and Dale. Don't say Henry, don't say Henry."

Prior to the ceremony, Bubba greets Dale and his parents and damn near introduces himself as Henry. Bubba is a mess.

Well, Bubba makes it through the ceremony without saying that name he wasn't supposed to say, even once. But then, he kept it short—about five minutes, so the odds of slipping up were smaller than if he had rambled on for a half hour or so.

Bubba dutifully signs the marriage certificate and heads straight for home. He grabs a piece of paper and drafts a letter, muttering to himself and writing furiously.

Bubba finishes his letter and reads it aloud to himself, "Dear Marriage Minister Company, I received the enclosed Marriage Minister Certificate from your company about two months ago. I feel compelled to self-report myself for drinking, smoking, swearing, chewing tobacco, and having impure thoughts and hereby surrender my Marriage Minister Certificate because I am sure that you will want to defrock me so I am no longer certified to conduct marriages in the state of South Carolina. Thank you, Bubba."

Bubba changes out of his ministerial clothing into his normal clothing and heads straight to the nearest bar for some Holy Water.

ooooo

Bubba is sitting at the bar, nursing a Bud Light and telling the bartender about conducting Holly and Dale's wedding and how he figures it took two years off of his life.

Bubba grabs his wallet from his back pocket and takes me from his coin compartment. He is deep in thought and nonchalantly flips me in the air and catches me time after time.

"What's with the penny?" a guy says as he sits down next to Bubba.

"Oh, I was just wondering if a penny comes up an equal number of times heads and tails if you flip it, say twenty times," Bubba says.

"Sure it does, it's the law of averages," the man says.

"Well," Bubba says as he gets ready to reel in the pigeon, "I'd bet you $10 that if I flip it twenty times, it will come up heads more than half of the time – more than ten times."

"You're on," the man says as he takes a $10 from his wallet and lays it on the bar.

Bubba places the penny on his thumb, face side up, and flips it. It comes up tails. Bubba continues to place the penny on his thumb, face side up for each flip of the coin, and when it has been flipped twenty times, the tally is heads 8 times and tails 12 times. Bubba loses his $10.

"Double or nothing?" the man asks.

"Sure," Bubba replies.

Bubba flips the penny twenty times and again he loses. He's now down $20 to the stranger.

"Go again?" the stranger asks.

"No, I've done enough gambling for one day. By the way, what's your name and where you from?" Bubba says.

"I'm Sheldon Myers from Bangor, Maine. I came to Goose Creek for the funeral of my best friend from high school who moved down here about twenty years ago. He was only forty-eight – much too early. His name is John Truman – did you know him?"

"The name sounds familiar, but I don't think I ever met him. Sorry for your loss," Bubba says.

Sheldon rises from the bar stool and says, "It's been a pleasure, but I've got a plane to catch."

Bubba replies, "Good talkin' to you – and here. . . . " Bubba flips me to Sheldon and he catches me in his hand.

"You earned it," Bubba says. "Good luck."

Farewell, Brother Bubba. You may not have been much at flipping pennies, but you were one helluva Marriage Minister.

The Wheels of Justice

I have a small drop of blood on me, on Abraham Lincoln's shoulder. I am in a plastic capsule about two inches in diameter and the capsule is in a sealed clear plastic envelope. I have been on the corner of this desk for the past three months and before that I was in a box with a bunch of other stuff in the Police Evidence Room for two months.

This is the office of the Assistant Attorney General of the state of Maine, Douglas Archer. There has been a steady stream of people in and out of the office discussing an upcoming trial and I have heard it all.

If only they knew what I know.

A person who I have never seen before enters the office and is greeted warmly by Douglas Archer. "Warren, thanks for coming all the way from Boston to play the devil's advocate for me. I want to present my case to you and I want you to see if you can poke holes in it, like a defense attorney will try to do."

"I'm ready," Warren says, "start at the beginning."

"It was Tuesday, August 24 of last year at 9:34 p.m. when this 911 call was placed. Listen to it," Archer says as he pushes the play button on a tape recorder.

"Hhhhelp me! Hhelp me! My wife is bleeding – she's been hurt – she's bleeding. . ."

"Calm down, please, sir – what is your name and your address?"

"Sheldon, 982 Orchard Circle – I'm Sheldon Myers,"

"Help is on its way. What happened to her?"

"I don't know – I just got home and found her like this - she's bleeding – I think she has a cut on her chest – I don't know."

"Is your wife breathing?"

"I don't know – I don't think so – there's blood everywhere."

"Have you tried to give her CPR?"

"I don't know how."

"I'll guide you. First, push down on the middle of her chest with the fingers of both hands. Push hard and fast 30 times, at the rate of two pumps per second."

(Pause)

"Okay, I did that, but blood comes out of her chest when I push. She has a big cut in her chest - Oh my God!"

"Okay. now, tilt her head back, pinch her nose, and cover her mouth with yours and blow until you see her chest rise. Do this two times."

(Pause)

"I tried it, I don't think it worked, she's still not breathing."

"Try pushing on her chest again and . . . ."

"Thank God, they're here – over here, help her, she's bleeding – she's not breathing, help her, oh my God!"

Archer pushes the Stop button on the tape recorder and

asks, "Well, what do you think?"

Warren says, "He sounds frantic. He's scared. He doesn't know what happened, he's in a state of disbelief and a state of shock."

"Bullshit!" Archer says. "He's faking it. He's way too dramatic – and he's a bad actor."

"He just discovered his wife in a pool of blood – how do you expect him to act?" Warren says.

"Okay, that's probably what the defense will claim, so I'll work on that. Now, the next thing is the detective's interview of him that evening. They took him down to the station and questioned him from 10:35 p.m. until 12:45 a.m."

"Did he ask for a lawyer?" Warren asks.

"No. But, watch the tape of the interview."

Archer pushes the button on a video recorder and the image of Sheldon Myers appears on a television monitor. He is alone in the small interrogation room. He is hyperventilating and it appears he could pass out any second. He bursts into tears and screams, "Why, why, why?"

A detective enters the room and offers Sheldon a cup of coffee. He takes the cup and takes a couple of sips.

"I am sorry for your loss, Sheldon," the detective says, "but I need to ask you a few questions to try to figure out what happened. Can you describe your activities of today and tonight."

"Well, I got up at my usual time, 6:47, this morning, took a shower, shaved, read the morning paper, ate cereal for breakfast, and left for work around 7:30. It takes about fifteen minutes to get to work, so I got there about ten minutes to eight, I suppose," Sheldon says.

"Where do you work?" the detective asks.

"Hammond Printing Company—we print calendars, advertising brochures – all sorts of business printing."

"What time did you leave work?"

"Oh, around 5:30," Sheldon says.

"Where did you go after work?"

"I went straight home," Sheldon says.

"What time did you get there?"

"It's about a fifteen minute drive, so I suppose about 5:45 or so," Sheldon replies.

"Then what did you do?"

"Well, I changed out of my work clothes into the clothes I'm wearing now and made myself a lettuce salad and a sandwich for supper," Sheldon says.

"What was on your lettuce salad?"

"French dressing," Sheldon says.

"And what kind of sandwich did you have?"

"Sliced turkey breast and cheese – you know, the kind with holes in it," Sheldon replies.

"Swiss?"

"Ya, Swiss."

"What did you have to drink?"

"A bottle of 7-Up."

"Was your wife home during this time?"

"No, she went out for a couple of drinks with her sister after work," Sheldon says.

"Do you know where they went?"

"I think they were going to go to Laughlin's — it's an Irish pub. Ask her sister, she'll know," Sheldon says.

"What's her sister's name?"

"Suzie McFarland. She's Tim McFarland's wife."

"What did you do after you ate your supper?"

"I always play poker with the guys on Tuesday nights at 7:00, so I left the house maybe around 6:30 to go over to Chris Hamilton's house," Sheldon says.

"Did you go straight there? Did you stop anywhere along the way?"

I stopped for gas at the 7-11 and then a few minutes later I stopped at the Country Store for a candy bar, and then I went to Chris's house," Sheldon explains.

"What kind of candy bar?"

"Snickers,"

"What time did you get to Hamilton's house?"

"A little before 7:00."

"Can you prove it?"

"Ask the guys - I walked in with Les, who got there the same time I did and Scott was already there," Sheldon says.

"What's the names of the guys you play with, besides Chris Hamilton?"

"Les Davis, and Scott Burleson,"

"What time did you leave?"

"We always stop right at 9:00 and I left shortly after that," Sheldon says.

"Did you go straight home?"

"I stopped at a McDonalds for a cheeseburger and a Coke and then I stopped at the 7-11 for a bag of pretzels, and then I went home and found. . . .I found Karen." And then, Sheldon broke down crying.

"Do you have any receipts from all of your stops along the way?"

Sheldon reaches into his shirt pocket and pulls out a bunch of receipts and hands them over.

The detective lays the receipts on the table in front of himself and puts them in order by the time stamp on each receipt.

"Mind if I keep these for a while?" the detective asks.

"No, go ahead," Sheldon answers, "but would you make me a photocopy of all of them, so I have a record too, in case I need them," Sheldon requests.

The detective agrees.

"Now, tell me about your wife's activities of tonight."

"Like I said, she and her sister were going to go out for drinks after work. She wasn't home when I got home from work or when I left to go play poker, and then when I got home after playing poker. . . .I found her. I don't know when she got home. Ask her sister, she can tell you. I dropped my wife off at work this morning and her sister was going to give her a ride home," Sheldon says.

"You failed to mention that before – that you gave your wife a ride to work," the detective says in an accusing tone.

"That was this morning – I didn't think of it at the time," Sheldon says. "It's been a rough night."

"Sheldon, were either you or your wife having an affair?"

"God, no! We loved each other. No!" Sheldon replies.

"Did you have a life insurance policy on Karen?"

"Yes, a $250,000 policy. When we bought the house, the loan officer suggested we each take out a $250,000 policy so if one of us died, the policy would pay off the house," Sheldon says.

The detective leaned in toward Sheldon and looked him straight in the eye. "There's one last question I have to ask you, Sheldon. Did you kill your wife?"

A look of surprise, and then shock, comes over Sheldon's face. "What? What? How could you possibly think that? I loved Karen. I would never do anything to hurt her. No, I didn't kill my wife, hell no, damn you."

"Well, that's all for now, Sheldon, we'll be in touch if we need any more information," the detective says.

Archer pushes the stop button on the video recorder and says, "Well, Warren, what do you think?"

"Did they check his body for cuts or bruises the night of the murder?"

"Yes, he had no cuts and no bruises," Archer replies.

"Did they identify what the murder weapon was?" Warren asks.

"We're quite sure it was a kitchen knife – there was a wood knife holder on the kitchen counter with a knife missing," Archer says.

"Did they find the knife?" Warren asks.

"No, they searched the house, garage, Sheldon's car,

and every dumpster between his house and Hamilton's house where the poker game was – he could have gotten rid of it a thousand places," Archer says.

"How many stab wounds did Mrs. Myers have?" Warren asks.

"We believe that she was first stabbed in the back twice and then she twisted around to face her attacker and she was stabbed one more time in the chest," Archer says.

"Did you check his clothes for blood splatter?"

"There was blood all over his clothes," Archer replies.

"Of course there was," Warren states. "His wife was covered with blood and he tried CPR – of course he was covered with blood. But was there splatter on his shoes or anywhere on his clothes that might have come from his wielding a knife and blood drops landing on him?"

"We didn't find any blood splatter on him or his clothes or shoes," Archer conceded.

"Well, then, it looks like you won't be able to score any points with blood evidence," Warren says.

"Maybe not," Archer says.

"How about his time table? Did they check security tapes at the places he stopped on his way to the poker game and back home again?"

"The times all match his receipts and they studied all the security tapes and talked to the store cashiers who were on duty," Archer says. "Here's his timetable. Look at it closely; see if you notice anything unusual – suspicious."

6:30 p.m. He leaves home for the poker game.

6:37 p.m. Time stamp on receipt for gas purchase at 7-11 for $15.78, paid by credit card.

6:43 p.m. He stops at the Country Store for a candy bar. It costs 99¢, tax included. He pays with a $1 bill and receives change.

6:55 p.m. Approximate arrival time at Hamilton's house for poker game.

9:00 p.m. Poker game ends.

9:05 p.m. Approximately time he leaves Hamilton's house.

9:13 p.m. He buys a cheeseburger and Coke at McDonalds. The cost is $5.50. He pays with a $5 and a $1 and receives two quarters in change.

9:26 p.m. He buys a bag of pretzels at the 7-11 store for $1.25. He pays for it with a $1 bill and a quarter.

9:34 p.m. He places the 911 call."

"That's very detailed, very specific," Warren says. "It makes for a strong alibi."

"Look at it closer, what do you see?" Archer says.

"I know what you *think* looks suspicious," Warren says.

"And, what's that?" Archer asks.

"He stopped more times going to and from the poker game than he needed to. He could have purchased the gas, candy bar, and pretzels at his first stop rather than stopping

149

a separate time for each purchase. Maybe he made this many stops to establish a tight time line for his evening – that's what you're thinking," Warren observes.

"Exactly, that's my point," Archer says. "Anything else?"

"You're also thinking, who takes the receipt for a $.99 candy bar and a $1.25 bag of pretzels and keeps the receipt?"

"Right!" Archer yells.

"From the defense viewpoint, forgetting something you were going to purchase, the candy bar, and stopping to pick it up later isn't a crime. Then, too, taking all the receipts and keeping them is the prudent thing to do. There's nothing in his actions that are even remotely suspicious or criminal," Warren says. "I don't think you can score points on either of these arguments. What else have you got?"

I interviewed the three poker-playing witnesses and the results were very, very suspicious," Archer replied.

"Suspicious in what way?" Warren asks.

"Each person's account of the evening is almost identical to each of the others, word for word, like it was rehearsed or memorized," Archer says.

"Or, their statements are similar because each of them is telling the truth," Warren says. "Each of them has a very simple story to tell – they met at 7:00 to play poker, they quit at 9:00, and the three of them left Hamilton's house and went home. That's why they sound similar. That's what the defense will say, and I think they're right."

"Okay, I'll work on that," Archer says. "but, let me continue.

"We interviewed Suzie McFarland, Mrs. Myers' sister. She picked up Mrs. Myers, the deceased, from her place of work at around 5:15 and they went to Laughlin's for a couple of drinks and dinner. She dropped Mrs. Myers off at her home at around 7:30. She went into the house for a few minutes and left and went home," Archer says.

"So, Mrs. Myers was killed sometime between 7:30 when her sister dropped her off and 9:34 when the husband, Sheldon, called 911," Warren says.

"The coroner believes it was around 8:00," Archer says.

"So how could Sheldon Myers have done it? He was playing poker with three witnesses who swear he never left to go anywhere between 7:00 and 9:00," Warren says. "By the way, did you give Sheldon a polygraph test?"

Archer hesitates for a moment and then he says, "Yes, we gave him two polygraph tests."

"And. . . .," Warren says.

"And, he passed them both," Archer says.

"Then why in the hell am I even here?" Warren asks. "He has a solid alibi with receipts accounting for his movements, he has three eye witnesses, and he passed not one, but two, polygraph tests. You are accusing an innocent man – this is a case you cannot win."

"The polygraph test results are inadmissible, so forget them," Archer says.

"They're pretty conclusive," Warren says. "He didn't do it."

"I have something else for you to take a look at before I

explain why I know Sheldon Myers murdered his wife – and how I can prove it," Archer says.

"When they brought Sheldon Myers into the station for questioning, they had him empty his pockets and wallet and they made an inventory of what he had—here's the list:

3 $20 bills, 1 $10 bill, 2 $5 bills, 4 $1 bills
2 quarters, 1 dime
Driver's license,
Emerald Hills Golf Club membership card
American Express credit card
Wells Fargo credit card
Social Security Card
Photo of his wife
A white handkerchief
A set of keys including the key to his car, his house,
    and his place of employment
Receipts for gasoline purchase for $15.78; candy bar,
    99¢; McDonalds, $5.50; pretzels, $1.25

"Warren, do you notice anything?" Archer asks with a voice full of apprehension.

"No, nothing unusual," Warren says.

"Well, I didn't either, at first." Archer says. "But then, after studying all of the information and evidence hour after hour, it hit me."

"What's that?" Warren asks.

"Look harder, see if you see it," Archer says.

Warren studies everything that Archer has presented. "I

still don't see what you're talking about."

Archer walks over to the desk and grabs the plastic bag containing the capsule that I am in. "This, Warren! This penny!"

"What in the hell are you talking about?" Warren asks.

Archer grabs the copy of the time line and points to the entry at 6:43. "Look, he bought a candy bar for ninety-nine cents and gave the clerk a dollar. He receives a penny in change, right?"

"Well, sure," Warren agrees.

"Now, look at the contents of his pants pockets and his wallet – do you see a penny among his possessions!" Archer exclaims.

"Well, no," Warren agrees.

Archer holds up the plastic bag containing me. "Don't you get it, Warren? This is the penny from his change when he bought the candy bar. Look at it – there is blood on the penny. Do you get it now?"

"Tell me," Warren says.

"Sheldon Myers slipped out of the poker game around 7:35 to 7:40 and went to his house to confront his wife about something, arriving there at about 7:55. For some reason, he took the penny out of his pocket that he got for change when he bought the candy bar and laid it on the kitchen counter. Then, he stabbed his wife to death with a knife and a drop of blood landed on this penny – the penny that he received at 6:43 at the Country Store. This penny is proof that Myers murdered his wife."

Warren looks at Archer with a stunned look on his face. "That's the damnedest most far-fetched story I've ever heard in my life. That's your case? Your proof? Do you think the jury is going to be a bunch of morons? You should give up practicing law and start writing novels, or maybe science fiction."

"You apparently missed the point," Archer says.

"Did you search his car for a penny?"

"We did and there was no penny in his car," Archer replies.

"But, he could have dropped the penny in the "Leave a Penny, Take a Penny" cup or it could have slipped out of his hand and fallen to the ground or he could have thrown it out of the window. There are billions of pennies out there – to say this one penny with blood on it is the penny Sheldon Myers received as change when he bought the candy bar is pretty far out there. In fact, it's crazy," Warren says.

"Wait until I tell my story to the jury, you'll see," Archer replies.

"Well, how do you explain his slipping out of the poker game for well over a half hour without the other three poker players noticing he's gone?" Warren asks with a smirk on his face.

"There's a simple explanation," Archer says. "They're all in on it with Myers."

"Huh?" Warren says. "Where in the hell did you get that idea?"

"Let me ask you one simple question, Warren – what are the two main reasons that a person murders their spouse?"

"Either one of them is having an affair, or for money," Warren responds.

"Right!" Archer exclaims. "Remember the $250,000 life insurance policy on Mrs. Myers – there's the money motive. My theory is that Sheldon Myers is cutting his poker-playing buddies in for $10,000 or $20,000 apiece for providing him with an alibi."

"Doug, Doug," Warren says, "all you've got is a *theory*, in fact, a whole bunch of *theories*. You don't have one shred of evidence that shows Sheldon Myers killed his wife."

"I believe that I have a very compelling story and a theory that works—and, I can be very convincing, as you know. I believe I can sell a jury on my theory and get a conviction," Archer says.

"Doug, Doug," Warren says, "I know Sheldon Myers is innocent, you know Sheldon Myers is innocent, and you're on the verge of trying to railroad an innocent man for something he didn't do. What's going on here?"

"My job as the prosecutor is to present my case as vigorously as I can, and it is the job of his defense attorneys to defend him as vigorously as they can, and then the jury will decide. If the jury decides that my case is a sham, they'll find him innocent. On the other hand, if they believe that my theory makes sense, well. . . ."

"Doug, I've known you for twenty years and I'm not buying that bullshit. Off the record, level with me—what the hell's going on?" Warren says.

Archer thinks for a moment and then he says, "Okay –

off the record, okay?"

"Off the record, agreed," Warren says.

"Two things," Archer says. "First of all, this is the biggest murder case to hit the state of Maine in maybe fifteen years. Hell, it's even made the national news. People are screaming for a conviction and the press has already convicted Myers in the media. Everybody is expecting a conviction—they're demanding it. That's why the case was removed from the District Attorney's office in Bangor and given to me here in the State Capitol – to make sure a high profile prosecutor – me – delivers the conviction.

"Still off the record – second, I have political ambitions. If I win this case, the sky's the limit for me. I could see myself getting elected Governor or maybe even becoming a U.S. Senator."

"Doug, remember the oath that you took when you were admitted to the Bar? Doesn't that mean anything to you to seek fairness and justice?" Warren asks.

"Of course it does," Archer says, "but to be honest, I'm in too deep to do anything than to plow ahead and see this case through. I've made too many statements to the media – made too many promises to back out.

"Besides, if my theory is as weak and unbelievable as you say it is, the defense will raise all the issues you raised and the jury might see it their way and Sheldon Myers will be acquitted. If that happens, I'll scream and holler and blame the defense attorneys for using dirty tricks and blame the Judge for screwing up the case and even blame the jury for being a bunch of weak-kneed idiots who couldn't see the truth. I'll still be able to use all of the publicity this case has generated for me to pursue my political career. So, you see, I can't lose.

"One more thing, if the jury does convict Myers," Archer says, "his attorneys will immediately file an appeal citing all sorts of reasons that the conviction should be thrown out or there should be a new trial. That might take two years and by then, I could be Governor or a U.S. Senator, and I'll be above it. And when the conviction is overturned, Myers will sue the state for millions. Everybody wins!"

"Doug, you're a real shit," Warren says. "I'm going to make one final statement and one final appeal to you and then I'm going to leave. For God's sake, stop this charade and dismiss the case citing lack of evidence. And if you can't do that, stick to the facts rather than making up these preposterous theories that have no basis whatsoever in fact. That's all I have to say."

If only they knew what I know. I am Archer's key piece of "evidence," and I will be in the courtroom to witness Archer's face when the jury finds Sheldon Myers innocent. That should be fun!

ooooo

Assistant Attorney General, Douglas Archer, presented his case in the murder trial of Sheldon Myers exactly the way he had laid it out to his friend, Warren. Around his office, he is cocky and arrogant, but here in the courtroom, he has a demeanor that seems to say, "Aw shucks, I'm just a country lawyer telling you a simple story of what happened the night Sheldon Myers murdered his wife."

Kimberley Fairchild and Clark Marshall are Sheldon Myers' defense attorneys and they have done a magnificent job of refuting every claim, accusation, and theory presented by Douglas Archer, exactly the way that Archer's friend, Warren, had predicted.

The prosecutor and the defense attorneys have both presented their sides of the case and both have given their closing arguments. The case is now in the hands of the jury.

ooooo

After deliberating for six hours, the jury sends a message to the Judge that they have reached a verdict. The jury files back into the courtroom. The Judge says, "Ladies and Gentlemen of the jury, have you reached a verdict?"

The jury foreman says, "Yes we have, Your Honor."

The Judge says, "Please read your verdict."

The jury foreman reads the verdict - "In the case of the State of Maine versus Sheldon Myers, we find the defendant. . . . guilty of murder in the first degree."

ooooo

Assistant Attorney General Douglas Archer has hoodwinked the jury.

If only they knew what I know. I can't tell the Judge or the jury, of course, but I have to get it off my chest.

Sheldon Myers returned home Saturday night, August 21, from attending the funeral of his high school friend in Goose Creek, South Carolina. His wife, Karen, had waited up for him and he arrived home around 11:00 p.m. She met him at the door with a hug and a kiss.

Sheldon told her all about the trip, the funeral, and some of his old friend's acquaintances that he met in Goose Creek and Charleston. He told his wife the story about meeting this guy, Bubba, in the bar and how he had won $20 off him flipping a penny. Then, he reached in his pocket and pulled me out and showed me to his wife. Then, Sheldon Myers laid me on the edge of the kitchen counter.

I remained on the kitchen counter while Sheldon and Karen Myers went about their daily routines in their home on Sunday, Monday, and Tuesday morning. They were a happy, loving couple.

Tuesday morning, Sheldon read the morning newspaper and ate cereal for breakfast exactly as he had described to the detective when he was questioned the night of August 24. He and his wife left the house together around 7:25 a.m. to go to work.

The rest of the day, I was in the house all alone until Sheldon Myers came home from work around 5:45 to change clothes and eat his supper consisting of a lettuce salad, a sandwich, and a bottle of 7-Up. He left the house around 6:30. Around 7:40 that night, Karen and her sister, Suzie, arrived. Apparently, they had been having an argument and it continued when they got inside the house.

"You've got to pay me back the money you borrowed," Karen

said. *"Sheldon doesn't know I loaned you twenty-five thousand dollars and he's starting to get suspicious. I've got to put the money back before he finds out. You know, after the last time, I promised him I wouldn't loan you any more money. You promised to repay it last month and the month before and the month before that—I need the money* **now!** *"*

"You said it was twenty-five thousand," Suzie said, "I thought it was only twenty-three."

"It's twenty-five," Karen stated firmly. "I've written it down every time you borrowed money."

"Just show me your record of the loans, and I'll write you a check for the full amount," Suzie said.

Karen disappeared into the next room and returned a couple of minutes later with a piece of paper. She handed it to Suzie and said, "See, twenty-five thousand."

"Okay, you're right, twenty-five," Suzie said. "Do you have another copy of this I can have for my records?" Suzie asked.

"No, this is the only copy," Karen said as she took the paper and turned her back to Suzie to walk away.

In a sudden impulse, Suzie grabbed a knife from the wood knife holder setting on the kitchen counter and plunged it into Karen's back. Karen stiffened up and Suzie withdrew the knife and quickly stabbed her a second time.

Karen managed to turn around, facing Suzie, and with a look of shock, horror, and disbelief she moaned, "Why?"

Suzie, raised her hand high and a drop of blood flew from the knife's blade and landed on me, right on Abraham Lincoln's shoulder.

Suzie drove the knife's blade deep into Karen's chest and Karen fell over backwards onto the floor, her eyes wide open, staring at Suzie.

"Why?" Suzie said, "Why? Because I don't have the money to repay you. You can't tell your husband you loaned me the money, and I can't tell my husband I borrowed it. I'm sorry, this was my only way out. I love you."

And then, Karen died.

Suzie grabbed a dish towel from the towel rack and wrapped the knife in it and she picked up from the floor the sheet of paper listing the amounts she had borrowed. Suzie looked around to see if she had left anything behind, and exited the house, leaving the door unlocked behind her.

If only the Jury knew what I know.

On the Fast Track

Sheldon Myers was convicted of murdering his wife on March 3. The winning prosecutor, Assistant Attorney General Douglas Archer, wasted no time riding his newfound wave of popularity to bigger and better things. In the first week after the trial's conclusion alone, he appeared on eight television programs in Maine, three national television programs, and a dozen Maine radio stations. There are fifty-nine newspapers in the state of Maine and every one of them ran a big story featuring Douglas Archer and some of them ran two or three stories that week. It is a fair assessment to say that Douglas Archer was the toast of the state of Maine.

As soon as the Sheldon Myers verdict was read in the courtroom, chaos broke out and, in the confusion that ensued, Assistant Attorney General Douglas Archer *stole* me from the evidence table. I have been in his left front pants pocket ever since and every now and then he holds me in his hand and talks to me like I'm an old friend, "You're my lucky penny— stick with me, we're going to the top."

I wish I had never met the miserable son-of-a-bitch.

Douglas Archer's timing was perfect – the Sheldon Myers trial finished just in time for Archer to file papers to run for the U.S. Senate seat that was being vacated by the retiring Joshua Horner, who had served honorably in the Senate for twenty-eight years.

Archer's opponent in the Senate race could just as well have saved himself a lot of time and trouble by withdrawing from the race as soon as Archer announced he was running. Archer won the Senate seat in a landslide with an unprecedented seventy-six percent of the popular vote.

ooooo

Senator Douglas Archer has a secret plan. He will quickly make his mark in the Senate by introducing several pieces of sweeping legislation that will gain him national attention and admiration. Then, after serving in the Senate for two years, he will run for President of the United States. His will be the most meteoric rise in the history of United States politics, from Assistant Attorney General to President in a scant three years. Look out, here comes Douglas Archer.

The only problem with Senator Archer's plan is finding an issue or cause to trumpet that none of the other Senators or Representatives haven't already thought about. What he needs is an issue that affects every American voter in their day-to-day lives and that also hits them in their wallet.

He was massaging me between his thumb and index finger, as he often does when he is thinking—after all, he does consider me to be his lucky penny. Suddenly, the idea hit him like a shovel in the face. He had his issue, and it was perfect. Every radio and television station in the country would discuss and debate his proposed legislation and he would be a household name within weeks. Pennies, that was the answer, Pennies!

ooooo

The U.S. Senate is in session and the Speaker has just recognized "The Honorable Senator from the State of Maine, Douglas Archer."

Archer is nervous. His right hand is waving all over the place and his left hand is in his pants pocket, massaging me for comfort and wisdom.

"I propose Senate Bill Number 1942-29-918: To eliminate the manufacture of the United States Currency known as the One-Cent Piece," Archer says.

What? He wants to eliminate the One-Cent Piece – eliminate Pennies? If I had teeth I'd bite him in the nuts.

Senator Archer continues, "My research shows that it costs two and a half cents to manufacture a One-Cent penny for zinc and copper raw materials, machinery, production, and labor. There are approximately five billion pennies manufactured per year and at a savings of one and a half cents per penny, that is Seventy-five million dollars per year that can be saved by eliminating the penny."

A Senator jumps to his feet and the Speaker says, "I recognize the Honorable Senator from the State of Alaska."

"You may be unaware, Senator Archer, but the state of Alaska produces over fifty percent of the zinc mined in the United States. A penny is 97.5% zinc, so eliminating the

165

manufacture of the penny would be detrimental to the welfare of the state of Alaska. I think it's a stupid idea."

Another Senator jumps to his feet and the Speaker says, "I recognize the Honorable Senator from the State of Arizona."

"Arizona is one of the leading producers of copper, which is still an important ingredient in the manufacture of the penny and eliminating the penny would hurt the Arizona economy," the Senator says. "I agree with my esteemed colleague from the great state of Alaska – you're nuts."

Senator Archer removes me from his pants pocket with his left hand and holds me up for the entire Senate to see. "It is time for the lowly penny to go," he says. "It has lost its value, it costs more to make than it is worth, and the United States Treasury can save seventy-five million dollars a year by halting production of the lowly penny."

A Senator with long white hair and a well-trimmed mustache and beard slowly rises and the Speaker says, "I recognize the Honorable Senator from the state of Kentucky."

The Senator from Kentucky slowly walks to the front of the senate chamber where Archer is standing and speaks in a slow southern drawl, "I commend you, Senator Archer on doing your research on the cost of making a penny and on finding out how many pennies are manufactured per year. That's good work."

The Senator from Kentucky is now three feet from Senator Archer and he holds out his hand, palm up to Archer. "I see you're holding a fine-looking penny in your hand,

Senator Archer; may I see it."

Archer hands me to the Senator from Kentucky, who turns and slowly walks back to his seat. He turns and faces Archer. He holds me high for all to see as he speaks, "One thing your research failed to show, Senator Archer, is that a penny is not just manufactured and used once and then thrown away. No, no. It is passed from one person to another to another to another for years and years and years and every time that penny is passed from one hand to another, it has a value of one cent. If it passes through a hundred thousand hands in its lifetime, why, that penny has had a value of a thousand dollars. And, if this penny I'm holding right here in my hand could speak, it could tell some amazing stories of the hands it has passed through and of the business deals it was a part of and of the things it helped people accomplish in their lives. It is not a lowly penny as you suggest; it is as much of American culture as baseball, apple pie, and University of Kentucky basketball. Mr. Speaker, I ask for a vote on the bill proposed by the Senator from Maine."

The Senator from Kentucky holds me out in front of himself for everyone to see and then, with a flourish, he puts me in his pants pocket.

Before the Speaker can respond, Senator Archer blurts out, "That's my penny, I want my penny back."

"Well," the Senator from Kentucky says, "I'm not going to give this penny back. You gave it to me and I'm going to keep it."

"I didn't give it to you, you took it and if you don't give

it back, I'll sue you," Archer threatens.

The Senator from Kentucky rises to his feet, withdraws me from his pocket, and holds me up in front of himself.

"Senator Archer," he says, "a few moments ago you described the penny as basically being so worthless that it should be eliminated from society but now, you're telling me that this single penny is so valuable that you would actually sue a United States Senator from the State of Kentucky to get it back. You have been talking out of both sides of your mouth, Senator. I know the value of a penny and I appreciate the value of a penny, and I'm keeping it."

∞∞∞

The Senate vote on *Senate File Number 1942-29-918: To eliminate the manufacture of the United States Currency known as the One-Cent Piece* was as follows: For, 1; Against, 96; Absent, 3.

∞∞∞

Douglas Archer wasn't the only person whose life was changed dramatically as a result of the Sheldon Myers murder trial. Archer's former friend, prominent Boston Attorney, Warren Wilkinson, was so upset by Archer's blatant mishandling of the case and with the conviction of a man who he knew was innocent that he took six months off from his law practice to write a book about it. The title of the book is *WHEELS OF INJUSTICE – THE CONVICTION OF AN INNOCENT MAN.*

Wilkinson analyzed every shred of evidence introduced by Prosecutor Archer, and shredded it. He interviewed witnesses that the detectives never even talked to. He gave polygraph tests to Sheldon Myers' three poker-playing buddies, and they all passed. He interviewed the bartenders and waitstaff at Laughlin's Irish Pub, where Karen Myers and her sister had drinks and dinner, and found that the two of them had been in a lengthy, heated argument – something about gambling losses and wild spending.

Investigation of banking records showed that Karen Myers had written over a dozen checks of varying amounts to her sister, Suzie McFarland, over the previous two years.

Wilkinson hired a forensic coroner to examine the angle that the knife blade wounds entered Mrs. Myers' body. He determined that the angle showed the person wielding the knife was no more than five feet five inches tall. Sheldon Myers is six foot two. Suzie McFarland is five foot four.

Warren Wilkinson did not identify who the actual killer was, exactly, but when a person finished reading the book, it was obvious that it was not Sheldon Myers – and it was pretty plain who it was.

WHEELS OF INJUSTICE became a "must read" for everyone in the state of Maine and became a sensational national bestseller. The public outcry for justice for Sheldon Myers was deafening.

ooooo

Douglas Archer wasn't the only attorney involved in the Sheldon Myers murder trial to run for public office, but the other person ran for a completely different reason than Archer's.

The lead defense attorney, Kimberley Fairchild, was so appalled by the tactics used by Assistant Attorney General Douglas Archer, and apparently approved by his boss, the Attorney General, that she decided to switch sides of the courtroom and run for Attorney General a year after Douglas Archer was elected to the Senate. Bolstered by the findings reported in Warren Wilkinson's book, she had a compelling argument: "If you were innocent and were charged with a crime, would you want an Attorney General who would decide you were guilty and railroad you to a conviction, or would you want someone who would seek the truth."

Kimberley Fairchild beat the incumbent Attorney General by fourteen percent.

ooooo

On her first day in office as Attorney General of the state of Maine, Kimberley Fairchild did three things. First, She filed a motion to have a hearing to consider the immediate release of Sheldon Myers from prison. Second, she ordered the reopening of the investigation of the murder of Karen Myers. Third, she charged Douglas Archer with *Prosecutorial*

Malpractice for his handling of the Sheldon Myers case.

ooooo

The Senator from Kentucky, Sherwin Scruggs, who saved billions of pennies from extinction that day in the senate chamber, never did give me back to Douglas Archer. Senator Scruggs had me framed and he hung me on a wall to the right of his desk in his office. Many times, people saw me and asked, "What's the story about that framed penny?" The Senator would delight in telling his story about how he had put the junior senator from Maine in his place that day and how he had saved the penny from annihilation.

From my vantage point in Senator Scruggs' office, I saw Senators, Representatives, lobbyists, ambassadors, heads of foreign countries, the Senator's constituents from Kentucky, the Vice President, and even the President of the United States come in and sit for a while over the five years I hung on that wall.

I heard deals made, deals turned down, legislative bills written, strategies planned, and lots and lots of stories, including a few about the love life of several people in congress. Through it all, Senator Sherwin Scruggs was an honest and honorable man.

ooooo

Senator Sherwin Scruggs served in the U.S. Senate for

thirty-three years, until he was felled by a heart attack at age 83.

His aides packed up his office and gave all of his mementos, including me, to his wife, who was twenty-one years younger than the Senator.

Mrs. Scruggs placed the urn containing the Senator's ashes on a table in her bedroom and stashed a couple of boxes of the Senator's favorite mementos, including me in my frame, in the corner.

Mrs. Scruggs mourned and grieved for her husband without hardly leaving the house for nearly a year.

When she received an invitation to attend her high school class reunion in Cheyenne, Wyoming, she decided it was time to reconnect with the world.

At the class reunion, Mrs. Scruggs reconnected alright, with her high school boyfriend who had been recently divorced. The old flame was re-ignited and the two of them decided to pick up where they had left off some forty-five years ago and to move to California.

Mrs. Scruggs returned to Washington D.C. and held a yard sale to sell everything that wasn't nailed down. She placed five dollars on the urn containing the Senator's ashes and a woman bargained her down to four dollars. She thought it would make a lovely flower vase. The fate of the Senator's ashes is unknown, but you can figure it out.

A young man bought me, and my frame, for three dollars.

When he got home, he removed me from the frame and

replaced me with his college graduation diploma. He gave me to his ten-year-old brother.

The following day, the ten-year-old brother took me along to school, where he flipped pennies with two other boys during the noon hour.

During the first class session after the noon hour, a stern-looking woman knocked on the classroom door and led the three penny flippers, with pockets filled with pennies, to the Principal's office.

Years ago, I was hauled into a Principal's office in the pocket of a penny flipper, just as is happening at this moment, and I know what's coming next.

Update

A lot of years have passed since that day when I made my second trek to a Principal's office in the pocket of a penny flipper.

I have traveled to every state in the United States, including Alaska and Hawaii and I have been to twelve foreign countries and back again, including twenty-three trips to Mexico and seventeen visits to Canada.

I have seen some amazing things and have met some interesting people of all ages and all walks of life. I've basked in the sunshine and I've been in the deepest of darkness. I've been prized and hungered for and, on the other hand, I've been scorned, ridiculed, pinched, squeezed, ignored, hoarded, stepped on, driven on by cars, and threatened with total annihilation and extinction, more than once.

I don't have enough time to tell you all of my stories, because it would end up as a book so large you'd have to haul it around in a wheelbarrow.

Next time you receive a penny in change, take a good look at it rather than just casually throwing it into your change drawer, purse, cup, or wallet. Ponder for a moment, the life that penny has lived, the hands it has passed through, the things it has seen, and the stories it could tell.

If the penny was minted in 1982 in Denver, it might just

be me that is in your hand. Treat me kindly, for I am special, you know. I was the final penny minted on October 22, 1982 and the final penny ever made of 95% copper with just a touch of zinc thrown in.

I don't shine as brightly as I did back in 1982, but then again, neither do you.

I have been here in this cash register drawer in the Black Bear Diner in Bullhead City, Arizona for about fifteen minutes. The drawer is opening and someone's fingers are reaching for me.

It's time to move on.

www.ingramcontent.com/pod-product-compliance
Lightning Source LLC
Chambersburg PA
CBHW051513170626
46811CB00002B/807